Fire in the Moonlight

Dria Andersen

To my husband, who was my sounding board, my cheerleader, my critique partner, and all the things I needed to finish this project. I appreciate every hour, every word of input, and most of all, your unwavering support.

To my family, who had to deal with mommy being on in another world for hours at a time. Thank you for your patience.

To my aunt Cathy who gave me my first love of romance stories, I thank you for allowing me to raid your bookshelf.

Thank you to every fan who continues to stick with me while telling the stories playing in my head. I appreciate each and every one of you. I would like to give a special thanks to A.K Edits for getting my baby ready for the world. I also want to shout out Shirelle and Rayshawnda for giving me so much encouragement when I was running out of steam. You guys are the BEST and I appreciate you!

Author's note

So, we've reached the end of the adventure of the Fouche cousins and while I'm a little sad, I'm happy that I was able to bring them to life. I think, even in the writing, you can get a small glimpse of my sadness to leave them. Lol Their world, though fictional is built around the town like the one I grew up in and it's a little bittersweet to let them go. Also, I've added family trees for both the Fouches and the Taylors. Now, bear with me because it was harder than I thought. It's not a complete family tree, it just includes the characters that appear in the three books so far. If I decide to explore the world a little more, then I will fill it out where relevant. That being said, I hope you guys enjoy the ride.

Content Warnings:
Death
Explicit language
Explicit sex
Occult subjects

Family tree

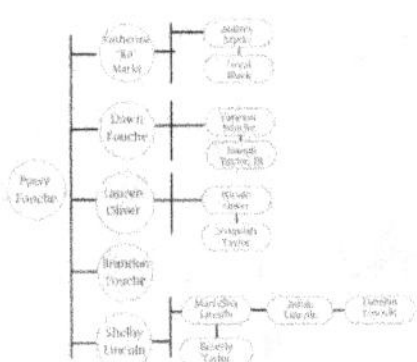

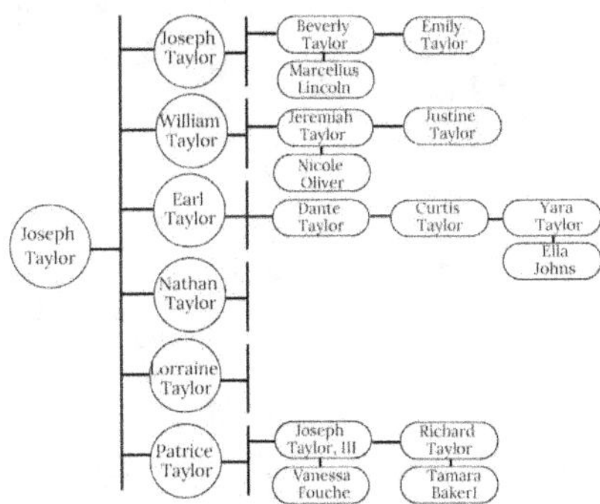

Prologue

There were a number of things Vanessa Fouche's grandmother taught her, the main one being to trust her instincts. Right now, they were screaming at her, telling her to move faster. The job had given her pause from the beginning, but despite most people's lies, there was always a number. A number that someone would do anything for. It just so happened that the amount of money this client had offered had surpassed hers.

She hadn't fully considered the consequences of the job or the fallout. Honestly, the summons from her grandmother's estate couldn't have come at a better time. She needed a place to hide, and a rural town in Georgia would be the perfect place, mainly since she hadn't used her real name in at least five years. Clients didn't give sensitive jobs to people with criminal records, so she'd been living as Olivia Wick for the last six years.

She didn't know how her grandmother's lawyers had found her, but she would count her blessings.

Ness rushed through the spacious room as she threw clothes into her suitcase. The floor-to-ceiling windows that she'd once loved were making her feel exposed and anxious. She didn't know how much time she had before they realized what she'd done and came after her.

Candace popped up in front of her. *"Hurry!"*

"How much time do I have?" she asked the spirit guide who'd been with her since she was a teenager.

Candace shrugged. *"He's powerful. I don't know if your spirits can hide you for long."*

Ness growled, the cat she and every woman in her family was cursed with roiling inside of her. The full moon was in a few days, and the animal would be harder to control with each day that passed. She looked around in irritation, knowing she'd have to leave everything else behind.

For the past four years, she'd lived in the luxurious high-rise, enjoying the fruits of her fraudulent life. The two-story condo had been her pride and joy, painstakingly decorated and filled with all the things she loved. She would miss it all, especially the clothes.

She tossed that thought, threw her cosmetic bag into her suitcase, and zipped it up. She didn't bother taking the elevator, rushing to the stairs. She'd replaced the heels she usually wore with practical sneakers, and the rubber soles were soundless as she darted down the seven flights.

"We'll make it," Candace assured her.

Ness rushed past the Porsche that sat in her assigned parking spot, heading instead for the beater she kept for emergencies when she needed to move unobtrusively. The small Honda was gray and nondescript. Though she'd lived on the straight and narrow on paper, she still dallied in other...not so legal things and needed to move around on the low. She started it, peeling out of the parking garage on her way to the airport.

Luckily for her, the ticket was in her real name and would be one less way she'd be tracked. In the airport bathroom, she carefully removed the thirty-inch wig that was a part of her Olivia persona. She carefully unbraided her hair and, using magic, fluffed it into a wavy crown, coloring it slightly. Sliding on her oversized designer shades, she took a deep breath. She was Vanessa Fouche again, and even though she was in incredible danger, that felt good. She would just pray that it was enough to keep her hidden. Besides, who would look for her in a small Georgia town?

Chapter One

Vanessa's leg bounced underneath the small table as she downed another shot. She'd been in Springbrook for a year and was just as stressed as when she'd arrived. Maybe even more so. Especially with the phone calls she was receiving. She had to figure out how to tell her cousins that the federal government may — or may not — be after them. The last call she'd received from one of her contacts in her old world was worrying. There was now a bounty on her head.

And not Olivia Wick's — Vanessa Fouche's.

When she'd run home at her grandmother's summoning, she assumed that even with the power to hunt her down, he wouldn't take the time to. This last call disabused her of that notion. How had the warlock found her? The bounty was a problem, but if Zane came here in search of her, it would turn the whole town on its head. She knew the Taylors wouldn't take it lying down, and she was almost certain her cousins would fight with their last breaths.

Ness felt guilty because it felt like she and her cousins had been fighting from the moment they touched down in Georgia. From the minute her grandmother's lawyers had found her, Nicole, and Audrey, what should've been a simple inheritance had turned into something much more complicated. In the time they had come home, they'd solved their grandmother's murder, found out Audrey had a secret husband, and rid their family of a centuries-old curse.

Breaking the curse months ago should've freed them from the last bit of danger surrounding the family, and here she was, bringing more.

Shit.

She sighed and waved at the bartender for another shot.

"You need to tell them." Her grandmother Patsy wavered into view to the right of Ness.

Patsy had been dead a good year but was chattier than ever. Vanessa looked up, and all the spirits she'd picked up in the last six months were staring at her in question. She sighed. She needed to get rid of them, at least the ones she didn't know. It was the ones she did know that were being bothersome, however.

"No need in getting an attitude with us," Candace said.

No matter what ritual she tried, Candace was a spirit that refused to leave her permanently. It wasn't until they'd found old pictures in her grandmother's safe that she finally figured out who the woman was. She'd been shaken to see a picture of the young woman in Patsy's things. According to some of the writings she found, the woman had acted very much like Ness. It was eerie. Long ago, her mentor had told her that a person could never tell which of their ancestors would watch over them, and Ness had finally understood that. Candace was a great-great-aunt that she'd never heard of, never mind met in her life.

"Please. Don't act like you don't need a guide," Candace inputted.

Ness rolled her eyes because that much was true. It was perfect, really, that the spirit sent was the one most like her. At times, it felt like Candace was trying to make sure Ness didn't make the same mistakes she had in life.

"Can I have a drink and think in peace, please?" she muttered to them.

A chill moved through her before her skin heated. She didn't even lift her head. Only one person could cause her body to react that way.

"Still talking to yourself, huh?"

She finally looked up, if only to sneak a peek at him. Square jaw dusted with a light beard, his mustache framing full, kissable lips and flawless skin, he was carved by God. Her stomach dipped before clenching. He was still so damn fine. His chestnut brown skin was glowing, or maybe it was just her.

The man had had years to notice her, and Ness could admit to holding a grudge that he hadn't. As she'd told her grandmother before, Trey was not checking for her. Why, then, did he insist on bothering her today?

She swallowed her drool and cleared her throat. "Don't come over here gettin' on my nerves, Trey."

He smiled, and okay...that smile still worked on her. She sighed and blamed her grandmother. Patsy had been calling him hers since she showed up months ago, making Ness reevaluate the man. Trey was a police officer and thus automatically struck off her list of people to get involved with. She may have long given up a life of crime, but some things were ingrained. So...he was off-limits.

It was best to keep her distance, mainly because she didn't want him digging around in her past.

Her grandmother scoffed next to her.

He sat down without asking, studying her with those inscrutable dark eyes of his. The puma within her went wild, her magic momentarily flaring out of her control. She gathered it quickly, especially when another spirit showed up behind him. And was that judgment she saw on the face of his ancestor? Either way, she couldn't afford more shades clogging up her magic. She exhaled, thankful when the bartender dropped two more shots in front of her. She could not deal with her traitorous body at the moment.

"You been in town a year and haven't been arrested once. Gotta be some kind of a record for you." He smirked. "What you sulking about?"

This fucking guy.

"I'm not in the mood, Trey. Move around." She threw back one of the shots.

"Awww, mama, tell me what's wrong so I can fix it." His eyes were sparkling with mischief, but his face was straight, his voice sincere. It was like he really wanted to fix it. That...

She took a deep breath because she was liable to fall for his game if she wasn't careful. "What you doing on this side of town? Didn't your mama ban you from this bar?"

He bit his bottom lip and eyed her. "Why you so mean to me, kitty cat?"

That fucking country ass twang coupled with his deep voice was finna get her in so much trouble. Lord, have mercy. Her hands shook as she cupped her shot glass.

He tilted his head. "How many of them you done had?"

She cursed the goosebumps sliding across her skin at his tone. It was just assertive enough to reach that place inside of her that she mostly suppressed. "That's not your business, deputy."

"Only 'cause you playing," he rebutted.

Her heart thudded, and her clit jumped — honest to God thumped against the seat of her yoga pants. Was he being for real right now? What did he even mean by that? Trey was potent, the wolf inside of him powerful and oh so very tempting...or maybe it was the four shots.

He held his hand up, and the bartender nodded at him. His eyes never left Ness, and she refused to lower hers. She knew the wolf would see it as a challenge, but she'd never been one to back down.

"You so fucking fine, Ness." He shook his head and licked his lips.

She diverted her eyes quickly or she'd give herself away. He didn't need to see the longing she knew was in her gaze. Trey claimed she'd been running, and yes, she'd been avoiding him, but her life was in shambles at the moment. It was for his own good.

He chuckled. "How you been doing, baby girl? I know there have been so many changes over by y'all."

The teasing had left his eyes. Empathy and concern coated his words, which were way more dangerous than his game.

"Answer the man," her grandmother taunted.

Ness closed her eyes and pinched the bridge of her nose. She'd never seen her grandmother this much when she was alive.

Patsy sucked her teeth. *"That ain't my fault. I'll be able to leave as soon as I get you straight. You my last grand."*

She barely restrained from rolling her eyes at the dramatic woman. According to Patsy, she'd managed to get all her grandchildren where they should be. Ness was the last holdout. But then, the others didn't have half the baggage she had.

"I need to go." She stood abruptly.

Trey smiled but didn't move. "I'll see you around, baby girl."

Everyone called her that. She was the youngest cousin, but damn if it didn't sound different from his mouth. She threw back her last shot and shuddered.

"You better not be driving either," he told her.

The dominance in his voice settled on her shoulders, and swear to God, she wanted to show this man her neck in submission. Trey was a problem.

"Find you some business, deputy."

She left the club and started the trek back to her grandmother's house. She'd run to the bar, hoping the exercise would help her organize her thoughts. It probably wasn't a good idea to chase that down with a couple of shots, so running back to the house was out. Hell, walking in a straight line probably was as well. She heard the roar of a motorcycle before it came up.

Dante pulled up next to her and stopped. "Baby girl."

Her body didn't so much as warm hearing the endearment from Dante. Ugh, Trey got on her nerves.

"I'm fine walking, Dante."

He looked her up and down in the tight yoga pants and cutoff tank she wore. "Yes."

She snorted. God, he was so sickening. "Who sent you to get me?"

"Sheriff Taylor," he said sarcastically.

Sheriff? When had he been promoted, and why hadn't he corrected her? God, that was even worse than him being deputy. What would she do if he got wind of the bounty on her head? She shivered and stopped walking, trekking over to Dante's bike.

He sucked his teeth. "I can't believe I been spitting all this game, and Trey got you out here feenin'."

She slapped his shoulder as she got on the back of his motorcycle. "Have you heard your game?"

He laughed. "Don't do me, shawty."

He waited until she settled before taking off. They were approaching her grandmother's land when she felt the magic settle over her. Dante cursed but drove through the barrier. They'd set it so that most of the Taylor gang could get through, but that didn't mean it would be comfortable for them. He dropped her off.

"Thank you, Dante."

"You're welcome, baby girl." He revved his engine. "Also, quit playing so hard to get with my cousin. He a good dude."

"Oh, you done mackin'?"

"*Mackin'*? Not you dug up that nineteen-eighties slang."

She laughed. "You get on my damn nerves."

"But nah, I ain't standing between—"

"Don't say it," she hissed.

He smiled, one reminiscent of Trey. All of the Taylors had that charming smile.

She turned away.

"Scaredy cat," he called after her.

She put up her middle finger, ignoring his laughter, and carried her ass in the house. She'd had enough of Taylor men for the day.

Chapter Two

There were a number of expectations put on the life Joseph Taylor the Third lived, but none more suffocating than the ones his mother upheld. Even as he played pool in the middle of the day with his favorite uncle, Patrice's voice was in the back of his mind, telling him that being seen on this side of town would be bad for his reputation. It didn't stop him from living his life, but sometimes...in the case of Vanessa Fouche, it made life a little harder for him.

Between his mother's rigid view of propriety and the job he held, courting Ness was proving tricky. He figured they could work past his job. His mother's disapproval would be trickier. Patrice was a God-fearing woman who attended church three times a week, and while his mother could tolerate some of what she called 'his bad habits,' getting together with a witch was not something she'd let slip. He defied the woman in many ways; pursuing Ness would be just another.

He mostly hid his doings from Patrice but had no plans to hide Vanessa. Nah, he fully intended to let the whole state know she was his...just as soon as he was able to catch her, that is.

He lined up his stick and dropped two balls while his Uncle Will cursed next to him. Trey chuckled and eyed the table to figure out what his next shot would be. The wolf within him was restless, but that was nothing new, so he ignored the animal. Until they had a certain woman underneath him, it was something he'd have to live with.

He looked up as sunlight spilled into the club from the front door. The motorcycle club his cousin owned was mostly empty, the lunch crowd already clearing, so nothing stopped his view of Dante as he swaggered back into the place. Dante found his gaze and nodded once, letting him know Ness had been deposited safely home. His wolf settled marginally, and he went back to his game. He could feel his uncle's stare across the table.

"So, you finna tangle with a Fouche, huh?" Will asked.

"Don't try to distract me from this ass whooping, Unc."

Will laughed. "You talking big shit for somebody that's gotta sneak on this side of town."

Trey snickered and sank another ball. "Not too much on my mama."

"My sister gon' throw a fit when you mate with a witch," Will warned him.

It was looking like a big 'if' if Ness had anything to do with it, but he kept that to himself. Besides, it wasn't like the whole county couldn't see how that woman was running from him. It was the main reason he planned to claim her loud and proud if she ever gave him the chance. For years, Vanessa Fouche had flitted in and out of town to visit her family, and while he'd heard of her, he'd never met her. Then one of the times she'd been arrested, her scent had reached him, and that was all it had taken for his wolf to latch onto her.

He'd taken one look at her and knew that he would need to make some moves in his life to be ready for her. So, while the pursuit of her was new, it hadn't stopped people in town from commenting on it and exaggerating the time he'd been chasing her. From the surprise on her face earlier, he clearly wasn't applying enough pressure. That would need to change.

Perhaps he'd been too subtle in his interest because Ness had yet to respond. That was alright. His wolf was nothing if not patient. He'd been keeping the animal from imprinting on that stubborn woman by the skin of his teeth. It was one of the reasons he'd never touched her. He feared that if he laid so much as a finger on the witch, it would be over for him and his wolf.

His control was contingent on him keeping his hands to himself.

"What up, cuz?" JT greeted as he approached them.

JT owned the motorcycle bar and was the current alpha of the Taylor pack. His cousin was only a year older than Trey, but that year translated to the power needed to be on top of the family. JT kept the Taylors well-fed, building on all the connections Will had established for the pack. Now, he was mated to a Fouche, and the pack's power had increased and was ringing bells all over the state.

In his line of work, Trey had his ear to the ground regarding power changes and laws that could affect his family. It was part of him doing his part for the Taylors. JT's work had all manner of people in the government talking. Trey diverted the attention where he could and passed on news when he couldn't. It kept his cousins out of trouble and made his job more manageable.

"Pop." JT dapped up Will.

"Nothing with me. Letting this pussy-whipped wolf beat me," Will grumbled.

"Letting? Oh, a'ight," Trey said, laughing, sinking yet another ball.

"I'm headed over to Ms. Dawn," Dante said, walking up with a round of beers. "I'm gonna go check on her if you looking for a way to get brownie points."

"Think that will work?" Trey asked.

He didn't believe that it would make a difference with Ness, but all the same, it would be a good idea to get to know his soon-to-be mother-in-law. He wasn't worried about brownie points, but maybe he could get tips from the woman.

Dante shrugged. "Ms. Dawn love me, but I don't know if she'll like you, so who knows?"

"Here he go," JT snickered, pulling out a backwood.

"What? I'm her baby, don't hate." Dante gave them a wide smile.

"I can't wait until you meet your mate. You too damn spoiled." Will shook his head.

"See how you do me, Unc?" Dante tried to take back the beer he'd brought.

"When you going?" Trey asked, finally missing the ball.

Will cackled and slid up to the table.

Dante shrugged. "I can hit you up before I slide through."

Trey nodded. He would move around his schedule so that he would be open. "Okay, I'll tag along."

JT lit his blunt and eyed him. "Auntie ain't gon like her."

"Let me worry about my mama," he muttered, knowing they were right.

Patrice had long ago made her feelings plain on the Fouches. Even before Trey set his sights on Vanessa, his mother had warned him away. He had a sneaking suspicion that she'd known they were mates long ago, but he kept it to himself.

"Ness was looking good today," Dante taunted. "I like when she on the back of my bike."

Trey couldn't help the spike of his wolf's aggression if he wanted to. He narrowed his eyes at Dante, knowing his cousin was trying to rile him on purpose.

The three of them laughed, with his uncle shaking his head. "I be forgetting how much power you hiding."

"Auntie Patrice the only reason he not in the hierarchy," JT commented with a shake of his head.

"Had to get a 'respectable' job," Dante joked, reaching for JT's blunt.

He could only shake his head because they weren't wrong. If she had her way, Trey wouldn't be anywhere near his cousins, so joining their motorcycle gang and wolf pack was out of the question. Unfortunately for his mother, Trey and his brother had already secretly joined. While he couldn't be a part of the hierarchy, it didn't stop him from being in the pack and participating in their runs and kickbacks.

On most days, Trey loved his job. He'd initially signed up for the Westport County Sheriff's Department to get his parents off his back. The job kept the Colonel from prying into his life, and his mother could gain the "respectability" she craved so much. Patrice's mission in life was to separate herself from her brothers and the Taylor name. According to his mother, the name carried weight in the state, but for all the wrong reasons. He'd been content as a deputy, but his wolf's natural inclination to be in charge had him making bigger moves. He'd run for sheriff in the last election and won in a landslide. His high school popularity translated to politics, and he'd used it to his benefit.

"You working tonight?" JT asked.

Trey leaned against the pool table. "I can be. You got a run coming this way?"

"Got some shit I'm moving out of the East Terminal. I know you got good deputies, but it would be better if you were there."

"Got it."

Trey could admit that many expectations came with the Taylor name; unbeknownst to his mother, he was fulfilling his part. He didn't consider himself a dirty cop so much as an undercover part of the Taylor MC. Their department was small, with maybe fifteen on-duty cops that covered the whole county. It was a lot, and for the most part, they kept the area safe. His deputies understood that some of that safety was bought by cooperating with the magic users in the area. They kept out undesirable paranormals, along with the wards the Fouches had long ago put over their town.

To that end, keeping both families happy was in the sheriff's department's best interest. They kept the county safe from outsiders and stayed out of the department's way. It was a symbiotic relationship that had been working for decades.

Trey hung out with his uncle and cousins for another hour before he called it quits. He needed to get some kind of sleep before he went in to help JT this evening. There was no telling how long it would take to offload everything. As was his habit, he drove past the Fouche land. He couldn't see their houses from the road, but it gave his wolf peace of mind. He needed a plan because his patience was running thin with his mate. Going with Dante would be a good start. Inserting himself into her life was a surefire way to get a reaction out of Vanessa Fouche.

Chapter Three

Ness lowered her head and hid her yawn behind the church fan she'd been lucky to find on the bench in front of her. It had sat neglected with an aging copy of a hymnal and a sturdy bible. She'd quickly realized why it was left there when it flopped as she tried using it. Her Aunt Shelby had given her a chastising look as she snuck in ten minutes ago. She waved to her cousins lined up on the bench behind Shelby and turned her body back to the front.

She adjusted the mermaid skirt she wore to sit comfortably. The gold polka dots on the skirt matched the gold high neck blouse she wore on top, but she regretted the amount of fabric that covered her body. It was demure enough for church, but the ceiling fans in this place were a joke, the struggling window units not doing much better. It was the middle of summer. Surely, there were better ways to church than this.

The door in the back opened a few moments later, to which her aunt sucked her teeth. Ness snuck a glance and snickered as Nicole walked in wearing over-large dark sunglasses and her hair in a pony-tail. Her lilac dress was beautiful and sedate, a belt cinching her tiny waist as the skirt fell into a waterfall of pleats. Despite their night before, Nic looked stunning and chic as she always did.

She slid into the bench next to Ness, the only seat left where their family was sitting. She had a feeling her Aunt Shelby had purposely put the two of them up here with her.

"What's the matter? Out being fast last night?" Ness whispered.

Nic stuck out her tongue and slid off her shades. Ness smothered a giggle at her cousin's tired eyes.

"That's the last time I'm going out drinking with you," Nic murmured.

"Liar," Ness scoffed, and they both giggled.

Aunt Shelby cleared her throat and cut a look at them that had them hiding their smiles.

"We need to talk after church. Don't think getting me drunk made me forget our conversation."

"That's not a Sunday conversation," Ness answered.

Nic hummed but dropped it.

"Heathens, the both of you, showing up late for Sunday school," their cousin Marcellus leaned up to whisper at them.

He and his family were on the row behind them, his wife's shoulders shaking as she hid her laugh.

Ness sucked her teeth. "I know your big head ain't talking. Your seat probably preheated for hell."

"Shh!" Shelby hissed.

Nicole gripped her arm as she smothered her giggles. Ness smiled and looked around, curious about the congregation her aunt was so faithful to. It was a small church with wooden benches and high ceilings reminiscent of every Southern church she'd attended. The pulpit was overflowing with the choir and musicians, all seated behind two pastors. There were two columns of seats, the rows full to nearly the back of the church. It was well-attended, but then, Springbrook only had one church, so if one needed saving in the area, this was the only place for that. She scanned the other side of the church, and low and behold, she saw a certain law enforcement officer. He wore a simple button-down open at the collar, the light blue color contrasting beautifully against his chestnut skin. He filled out the shirt in a way that hinted at the muscles beneath.

Her hands itched to touch him.

She couldn't see his pants, but she was suddenly anxious to see all of him. Lifting her eyes from her perusal, she collided with his onyx ones. He gave her a smile that had her squirming in her seat. The man was dangerous. She moved her gaze away and caught sight of his mother. Ms. Patrice's lips were pursed in displeasure as she noticed Ness eyeing her son.

"Mmhmm," Nic hummed next to her. "That's why you in here."

Ness snapped her gaze to Nic. "If you must know, I promised your auntie I would come."

"You must want something," Nic said.

Ness wanted that caramel cake recipe, but damn if she would say that and prove Nic's point. Instead, she flicked her wrist, the floppy fan extra irritating. Heat crept up her neck as she felt the sheriff's eyes. She darted her gaze back to him. He licked his lips, and heat bloomed throughout Ness's abdomen. Lord, the thoughts going through her mind in this church would send her straight to hell. She nodded toward the pulpit with a pointed look, and Trey's answering smile did nothing to quell the heat.

The man was a menace.

She just knew it.

His mother mugged Ness, and she turned her head. "Chile," she murmured under her breath.

Nic chuckled lowly next to her.

Their Aunt Shelby sucked her teeth and shushed them.

"Alright now, Auntie," Nic fussed.

Ness had to turn her head before she got popped for laughing again. She could hear Cellus and Bev both chuckling behind them. Her cousin was so damn ornery. She already knew their auntie was finna cuss every last one of them out as soon as the service was over.

The service wasn't as long as she'd been dreading, but it was long enough, considering she'd spent the bulk of it trying to avoid looking across the aisle at Trey. As soon as the pastor dismissed them, she hustled from the bench, already knowing Shelby was hot like fish grease. Ness popped Cellus on the shoulder when he stepped in front of her.

"You a hot mess," she snapped, tucking her smile.

"I ain't the one talking during service, baby girl," he laughed.

"All y'all should be ashamed. The kids acted better than y'all," Shelby said, gathering her grandkids and leading them to the back of the church and the exit.

Remembering that she needed her aunt in a good mood to get that recipe, Ness stuck her tongue out at her cousins and rushed to her aunt's side. She linked her arm with Shelby's and leaned her head on her shoulder.

"I'm sorry, Titi."

"Mhmm," Shelby hummed. "All that noise."

Ness laughed because her auntie was not finished fussing. Shelby sucked her teeth and mushed Ness's head, sending her cousins behind her cackling like they weren't next to be cussed out. Her heart expanded. Every day, she was more grateful to be home. It felt good to do this with her family after so many years of everyone being scattered about. She was looking forward to Sunday dinner for that reason alone. She'd missed so many over the years.

Ness squinted as they walked into the afternoon sun. The congregation was gathered, talking in small groups and catching up on a week's worth of gossip. Unbidden, her eyes sought out Trey. She thought hanging on her aunt's arm would deter him, but as soon as he spotted her, he marched his fine ass over to them. The slim-fitting navy slacks he wore left nothing to the imagination, and really, he ought to be ashamed to have worn the whore pants to church. Ness fought really hard not to drool as he got closer. His smile was all beautiful straight white teeth and dimples as his gaze traced her body. Her stomach clenched in reaction. He was so damn gorgeous.

"Morning, Ms. Shelby," he greeted her aunt, but his eyes never left Ness.

"Hey, Sheriff." Her aunt smiled at him.

The dark spice of his cologne seemed to surround her. Ness closed her eyes as notes of velvet rich vanilla assailed her. It was one of her favorite scents. She opened her eyes, and her breath caught at his nearness. His dark eyes seemed to see beyond her outer layer and directly to her soul. It was unnerving, and yet she stood trapped in his gaze.

"Morning, Vanessa."

She shuddered at his deep voice, barely able to find her own to mutter a greeting back. "Joseph," she managed after a few swallows.

The heat between them was undeniable, and it was getting harder for her to ignore every time they were in the same place, which seemed to be happening more than usual. Everything in her body craved him.

"Joe, let's go!" his mother called behind him.

"You're being summoned," Ness said softly.

He smirked at her, and even her magic responded. The man was trouble. She watched him walk off, licking her lips. She needed...

Lord, she needed to get her mind out of the gutter. She separated from her aunt. "What time dinner starting, Titi?"

"Aht-aht, you finna come help cook. Now that you're back, we don't have to endure my favorite daughter's new take on Southern foods."

"Now, Mama, why you do my baby like that?" Cellus asked.

Bev rolled her eyes and smiled. "Mama knows she likes my food."

"Now, you did manage to make kale palatable, so I'll give you that," Shelby teased.

Ness was so happy to be home.

"Titi…"

Ness gave an exasperated sigh as she failed once again to put out the fire she herself had started an hour ago. They were practicing in her Aunt Shelby's backyard, and Ness was about at the end of her patience.

"Don't Titi me," Shelby fussed, hands on her hips. "You need to get better at practical magic as an outlet for all that power inside you. Pretty soon, you gone have shades following you all over the place."

"I done told her," Dawn chimed in from the back porch.

Ness shot her mother an irritated side-eye. She wanted to say something, but the women were right. Shades differed slightly from the other spirits following her in that they didn't want to be sent to the spirit realm. They tended to be a little more aggressive and more of a drain on her magic. So, while aggravating, their advice was sound.

Ness returned to the fire contained within the magical circle her Aunt Shelby had built. She was having a hard time concentrating. She wanted to blame it all on the fact that a powerful warlock may or may not be after her, but honestly, most of her thoughts were consumed by one wily wolf. Just getting the picture of how he looked in church this morning out of her mind seemed impossible. There were so many reasons the man was wrong for her, his job being the top one.

Considering she was already tangled up with one law enforcement branch, getting involved with an officer of another seemed like asking for trouble.

Shelby sucked her teeth and put the fire out herself. "Niece, if you don't want to concentrate, then we can get out of this hot ass air."

"I'm so sorry, Auntie." Her shoulders drooped in defeat.

"What's on your mind?" Dawn asked.

"A wolf," Nic answered, coming outside with a tray of iced tea.

Ness grabbed a glass. "Ain't nobody ask you shit, Nicole Taylor."

"Ugh! Stank." Nic laughed, sitting down on the step next to Dawn. "You see how she talk to me, Auntie?"

As usual, her cousin didn't take offense to her bad attitude. Nicole was touchy about a few things but shows of pique and anger were never it. In the year that they'd been settling in Georgia, she was getting closer to her cousin, and they were finally in a place where they were comfortable with each other. She used to think Nicole was mean, and sometimes she still could be, but Ness had come to understand that her cousin was just never one to sugarcoat shit. She could appreciate that every now and then. Ness could admit that sometimes she let her temper flare. Where Audrey would try and soothe her, Nic simply cut to the heart of it, uninterested in the theatrics.

Dawn laughed. "I don't know who she got that attitude from, Nic."

Shelby rolled her eyes. "You better move before you get hit by lightning, Nicole."

They all laughed, and Ness relaxed into the comfort of her family. She sat on the step below her mother.

"Why weren't you in church this morning, Ms. Fouche?" Ness asked Dawn.

"I talked to God this morning when I woke up. At ten a.m. like a normal person," Dawn answered, wrapping her arm around Ness's shoulder, settling her between her legs. "We want to talk to you."

Her heart thumped. Did they know? "About what?"

"The house," Nic said.

Ness breathed out easier. "What about it?"

Nicole shared a look with their Aunt Shelby. "We've decided that it should be yours."

Her throat clogged. "Grandmother left it to all of us."

Patsy Fouche had died a little over a year and a half ago, leaving a successful microbrewery and her house to her three granddaughters. When Ness had first arrived in Georgia, she thought the three of them would live in their grandmother's house together, but now that Nicole and Audrey were mated and married, plans had changed. Still, she hadn't expected them to give her sole ownership. She was touched beyond belief.

"JT is building a place for us; quite frankly, the house seems suited to you. I can't quite describe it. It feels like yours," Nicole told her.

"Nic," she whispered, overwhelmed.

"Audrey agreed, and the sisters have as well," Nic told her.

Ness reached around her mother and pulled Nicole into a hug. She held tight to her cousin, touched beyond belief. She turned her gaze to the direction of the house and looked through the trees separating it from her Aunt Shelby's with new eyes. She'd always loved her grandmother's house and loved it even more with the changes Patsy had made before she died. She would enjoy making it more her own. She could even see having her own family here. That thought circled her back to Trey, and her stomach fluttered in nervousness. Why did the thought of family come back to him?

Lately, her thoughts had been straying to what she wanted to do with her life now that she was home for good. She helped Audrey at the brewery, which was all well and good, but she wanted something for herself. Their giving her the house seemed to align with those thoughts. Confirmation she was on the right track, perhaps?

"We should celebrate," Nic told her, done with sappiness.

Ness wiped her eyes and chuckled. "Want to go to Lore later this week?"

Did she want to get a glimpse of Trey? Perhaps, but that was her business if she did.

Chapter Four

For a Thursday night, Lore was jumping. The parking lot was full of both motorcycles and cars. Ness had kept it simple: a corset top, cut-off shorts, and a pair of high-top dunks in peach to match her top. Her silk press was still smooth, but all the same, she'd scooped the long strands into a high ponytail. In lieu of a full face of makeup, she'd painted her lips red and done her brows and lashes. She pretended that she wanted to look chill, but she'd put in the effort in case she ran into a certain new sheriff. She swung the tiny crossbody holding her ID and cards across her chest and exited the car.

She knew Nicole would be staying upstairs with her mate, so that meant Ness needed to be sober to drive herself home. She already missed Audrey and the fact that she'd moved to Savannah. Audrey was always down to be the designated driver. Ness smiled at the wolf at the door, who waved them in without checking them over. She pursed her lips when they stepped inside and saw the crowd. There were hella people in the bar.

Unable to help herself, her eyes immediately swept the area until they landed on the man she pretended not to notice. Her pulse was rapid as she spotted him leaning over a woman Ness had never seen before. She shouldn't care; it wasn't like she had any claim over the man, but it didn't stop her cat from prowling her body in restless switches. A slow tumble of her stomach was her signal from the cat that it was displeased. She purposely turned her head and body away.

Trey could talk to whomever he wanted to.

She wanted to ask Nic who the woman was, but she also didn't want to bring the fact that she was scoping Trey to her cousin's attention. Nicole was already teasing her about him. She wasn't in the mood for it. Ness spoke to some of the wolves she knew as they made their way to the bar. Finding a table in this crush would be impossible.

She greeted Emily at the bar. "I'm driving tonight, Em," she said as she settled on the stool.

"Sweet tea or soda?" Emily asked, knowing Ness well.

"Tea, please." She smiled and glanced back at the same spot she'd seen Trey.

He was still standing way too close to that woman, but that was not her business.

Nope.

Not at all.

Nicole caught her gaze as she looked back and snickered.

"Don't start," she fussed.

Nic raised her hand. "I ain't say shit." She turned her attention to Emily. "What's the deal with all these people?"

"Some big golf thing on the island," Emily answered, dropping a beer in front of Nic and a sweet tea in front of Ness. "Y'all eating?"

"Wings, please," Ness said, getting happy. She loved the wings here.

"Same for me," Nic told Emily before turning back to observe the room. "I wonder why they not partying on the island, then?"

"The island" referred to a small chain of islands sitting off the coast of Georgia. They held resorts, boating clubs, and a world-class golf course along with some of the county's richer occupants. It was rare for people who frequented the island to mix in with the locals on the mainland.

"Girl, you seen how much beer costs over there." Ness shrugged. "Plus, sometimes a good dive bar is what you're in the mood for."

"Fair." Nic cut a side look at her. "So, we gone pretend—"

"Yes, the fuck we are," Ness cut Nicole off. As far as she was concerned, she didn't see Trey.

Her cousin cackled and sipped her beer.

Trey knew the moment Ness crossed the threshold of the bar. His wolf went on high alert, and his body warmed. He searched her out and saw her moving toward the bar, her cut-off shorts showcasing them pretty ass thighs. The top she wore had her titties sitting, and damn if he could stop his eyes from following her from the door all the way to her seat at the bar. The woman he was chatting with was prattling on about the golf tournament she was involved in. He'd been playing wingman to Dante and was responsible for keeping the friend occupied. The woman was beautiful, but because she wasn't Ness, his wolf was way uninterested, the man even more so.

Dante was finna be mad, but Trey was done. "Excuse me, shawty."

He walked away before she could respond. He could never not answer the call of Vanessa Fouche. Scenting her over all the other smells in the bar, he slid behind her, smiling at Nicole.

"How you doing, baby girl?" he whispered in Ness's ear.

She stiffened but kept her gaze on the wings in front of her. Trey wanted to touch her, but he kept his hands to himself. He moved around to stand next to her instead.

"Not you over here disrespecting your date," Ness finally scoffed.

"I don't know that shawty," he defended himself, leaning back on the bar so he could see Ness's face clearly.

Goddamn, she was beautiful.

"Yeah, tell me anything," she snapped, returning to her food.

"What's going on, Trey?" Nicole spoke.

"Not much, Nic." He held out his fist, and she tapped it before resuming eating. "Talk to me, baby girl. How was your day?"

Ness studied him. "What do you want, Joseph Taylor?"

He snickered. "I can't just make conversation?"

"I don't talk to cops."

He placed a hand over his heart. "You do me so wrong, mama." He couldn't resist sliding a finger across the soft skin of her cheek. He shuddered as that small touch filled him with longing. "You keeping me at arm's length, and I don't like that."

She rolled her eyes. "I don't even be thinking about you like that, Trey."

The sharp tang his wolf associated with lies wafted around them. He grinned. "Who you trying to lie to? Me or yourself? Don't matter, though..." He leaned in until his lips grazed her ear. "I think of you enough for the both of us."

That was two touches. A dangerous game, but damn if he could stop himself. He slid her bar stool closer to him as he pulled back.

"Excuse you," she said, but he could see the pulse at her neck thundering.

His wolf whined, wanting to mark her so badly he could taste it. "I want to take you out, Ness."

She scoffed and wiped her hands off. "No, thank you."

He smiled, not at all discouraged by her automatic rejection. As fine as Ness was, she never lacked for males walking up on her. He was sure she'd developed all sorts of mechanisms to dissuade attention. But, in his case, she could say what she wanted — between his wolf and her puma, they both already knew what was up. The question was how long he'd let her get away with running from their mating.

"Why not?" He genuinely wanted to hear her reasoning.

Everything in him was protective of her, whether she wanted it or not. He wanted to alleviate her fears if it was just that, but the impulse to help her would override all his teasing if it were something deeper.

She shook her head and sipped from her drink. "We won't work, Trey. You're you, and I...got way too much going on to entertain you. Find you one of these good church girls to push up on."

"I don't want them. I want you." He watched her pupils dilate, heat entering her gaze. "Not to mention, my wolf ain't settling for anyone but the incomparable, sexy-as-hell Vanessa Fouche."

Her lips twitched, and she looked away as she fought a smile.

"You want me to quit my job for you?"

She gasped and swung her gaze back to him. "Trey, that's not..." She sucked her teeth when she realized he was joking. "You get on my nerves."

He laughed. "Since you won't let me take you out, dance with me."

Her eyes widened, and she licked her lips. "That's definitely not a good idea."

He sipped from his bottle. "You right. My shit bricking up just thinking about your hips moving on me. Especially in them damn shorts."

Her jaw dropped before she gathered herself back under control. That small glimpse of shocked pleasure showed him that Ness was not as worldly as she portrayed herself. The puma lit her eyes, and he could see the power of the animal moving beneath the surface. It was going wild. His wolf wanted to explore that power, but he pulled it back. His phone buzzed in his back pocket. He pulled it out and sighed at his mother's name. Ness eyed him with curiosity.

"Gotta get that, Sheriff?"

"Your mother-in-law calling. Give me a second," he teased.

"Boy, gone," she murmured, a blush heating her skin.

He smiled and walked outside to take the call. Last thing he wanted was for his mother to hear all the noise in the back. The woman seemed to have a sixth sense for when he was doing some shit she disapproved of.

"Mama," he greeted.

"Joseph."

It was all she said, but he felt the full weight of her irritation in that one word.

He sighed. "Mom."

"I know you can't help who your wolf chooses, but Jesus Christ on the cross, a Fouche?" She sucked in an aggravated breath. "I...I'm already tired of hearing your daddy's mouth about it. I done told you about even being on that side of town, and not only did you go behind my back and hang out with them hooligans, you went and attached your name to a Fouche."

Trey didn't bother defending himself. He knew she was on a rant and would let her wear herself out. He wished he'd brought his drink with him, however. He stared out into the darkened night, watching the cars leaving the parking lot as she droned on in his ear. Though he wasn't on duty, it didn't stop his vigilance.

"Joe!"

"Yeah, mama?"

"Are you even listening?"

He pinched the bridge of his nose. "Yes. You're embarrassed to walk into prayer service tomorrow. I can't do nothing about that. I done told you to quit letting them ladies shame you. I can probably pull a file on most of 'em."

Patrice sighed. "It be the ones in the most mess that's vocal too, but I don't be wanting to gossip."

He snorted at that lie but was happy about the subject change.

"Your father wants you home for Sunday dinner. He's not happy about this."

"The Colonel will be alright," he told her.

His mother sucked her teeth because she'd been unsuccessful in getting her firstborn to react as usual. No matter the hysterics, Trey had learned not to let his mother's anxiety rain down on him. For a while, they'd been stuck in a pattern of it. She'd reach out to him, spiraling from anxiety, and it would have him and his wolf in a state. It had taken his first panic attack to nip that in the bud. Now, he let Patrice rant, keeping himself separate from the emotions she provoked.

"Your brother and his mate will be there..." She left the sentence hanging.

He laughed. Wasn't no way in hell he was inviting Vanessa Fouche to his mama's house until he had her firmly mated and possibly pregnant. He refused to allow his parents to attempt to run her off.

"That's all you wanted, mama?"

"If you don't want to listen to reason, the least you could do is let your father and I meet with her."

"No, ma'am," was his answer to that.

She sighed. "Just be careful, Joe. And don't think I can't hear those motorcycles in the background. I done told you how them Taylors are."

"Mama, *we're* them Taylors, if you'll remember," he poked.

Though she referred to the Colonel as his father, he was technically Trey's stepfather. His uncles had run his biological dad clear out of the state because he couldn't keep his hands to himself. Trey had long suspected that the man was dead and buried somewhere in all this marsh, but he'd left it alone.

His mother had met her mate when Trey was barely five, so Franklin Harvey was the only father he knew. He'd wanted to adopt Trey, but one thing about Willie and his brothers, they didn't play about family, and as far as they were concerned, their nephew's name was fine the way it was. He'd been named after their father, and they wouldn't allow it to be changed.

The Colonel had raised him as his own under his strict regime, but Trey's uncles had made sure — despite their sister's protests —

that they were in Trey's life and understood the legacy that went with their name.

The Colonel had put his foot down with his second child, and Trey's brother had operated within the lines their daddy had drawn. Trey certainly wouldn't be the one to tell their parents that his little brother was washing money for the Taylor MC because then he would have to tell them his "police" job was more gatekeeping than actually enforcing the law. Not that he didn't do his best to keep the town and its citizens safe. It just looked different than the average policing.

Music spilled into the still air as the club's front door opened. Trey's wolf moved through his body as he spotted Ness sashaying out into the night.

"I gotta go, mama."

"Fine." Patrice let out an aggrieved sigh. "I love you."

"I love you too," he assured her.

His mother was high-strung and did everything she could to toe the line for her mate, but after years of dealing with it, Trey knew how to maneuver around her. He loved that woman but refused to let her spin him up whenever she called with a problem.

"Aye, shawty," he called out.

Ness whipped her head around, her eyebrows bunching at being catcalled. Trey smiled as she rolled her eyes.

"I thought your mama had called you back home," she taunted, walking closer.

He waited until she got within touching distance before he snaked his hand out and pulled her into his chest. He leaned against the side of the building, bringing her in between his parted legs. He rubbed their cheeks together. It was the first time he'd allowed himself the pleasure of full-on touching her, and it did not disappoint. Unfortunately, his wolf did precisely as predicted, wrapping its power around her, wasting no time marking her with his scent.

"Mama called because she heard about us," he told her, lowering his head to her shoulder. He nuzzled into her neck, pulling her scent into his lungs.

"Ain't no us," she shot back.

"So you say," he murmured against her skin. "You smell good as fuck, baby girl. I can't even think when I'm this close to you."

He peered down at the cleavage her top showed. Of course, his shit got hard. She was a work of art.

"You doing too much, Trey," Ness warned him.

He cupped her chin, lowering his head until their lips nearly met. "Why you giving me such a hard time, kitty cat? I know you feel this between us."

"You just looking for something to fuck on," she scoffed.

"Nah, you got me wrong. My wolf is involved, and he doesn't let go when he chases something down."

Unable to resist, he closed the distance between their mouths and initiated the first kiss between them. It started softly as he just wanted to feel the softness of her lips against his, but then she went up on her toes, and everything in him was pulled beneath her tow. The first taste of her dragged him under. He wanted nothing more than to bury himself in her. He already had feelings for her, that was part of the mating, but this... He could easily feel his heart melting.

The feather-soft strings of connection wound around her as his animal imprinted. Her magic responded, allowing the temporary binding. His wolf wanted more, filling his body until fur slid along the back of his neck.

She panicked and pulled back, her eyes searching his. He saw the knowledge of what they were there plainly. He also saw her fear. He could partly understand. The tumultuous emotions rioting through him blotted out everything else. Anyone would be scared by something that overwhelming. He stared into her eyes, and something about it triggered her magic. The cool breeze of it flowed over his body, and he felt himself falling into her gaze.

He saw the two of them battling, but not each other. They were fighting something else, something dangerous as the world around them erupted into flames. Her power was so great that he could nearly feel the heat of the fire. His wolf reacted as though the threat was real, a growl rumbling his chest. He would protect her from hell itself if needed.

Ness pulled back, stepping from his arms. "I can't... I have to go."

He could only watch her leave, his body trembling in both need and worry. He couldn't even process the images that had flashed between them. Was it the actual future? Was it a part of her power? Did he need to worry about some danger to the town? He wanted to chase her down to ask, but that wasn't his way. Trey was never impulsive. He didn't move without considering all the angles of a problem, and if what he'd seen was real, he needed to be very careful.

Chapter Five

Trey stretched his legs, settling into the low-slung chair on this front porch. He was tired as hell, but sleep had evaded him all night as the nightmares he'd seen in Ness's vision played through his head. He was worried about the town, yes, because that was his job, but his wolf's only thought was for their mate. Was she in danger? The animal was damn near begging at this point for him to go to her. All the patience he'd built over the last few years was crumbling.

If she was in trouble, all bets were off.

He wouldn't be able to keep from claiming her if only to keep her safe.

He stood as Dante pulled into his yard in the beat-up pickup truck he used for errands. That meant they'd likely be doing yard-work for Ms. Dawn. He didn't mind either way. Like he'd told his cousins, he wasn't riding for brownie points. Ness's family was important to her, and he needed her to know it would be the same for him. He could've introduced himself to her mother at any point since she'd moved back, but he knew how his mate felt about cops. He didn't know if her mother held the same disdain.

"What it do, Sheriff?" Dante greeted when he hopped into the truck.

"Ain't shit. What we doing today?"

"I never know. But she just moved in, so she probably got shit that need moving around," Dante answered, swinging his truck down the dirt road next to the main one.

The whole town of Springbrook was a series of intertwining dirt roads, a remnant from when its paranormal population still had to hide from humans. They seldom took the main road. It took less than ten minutes for them to get to the Fouche territory. Dante cursed as they crossed over the magical barrier that protected the property.

It was uncomfortable, but it had never been as bad as his cousins experienced. A part of him wondered if they were exaggerating or if there was something that allowed him through without trouble. That perked him up a little. Was it his connection to Vanessa that protected him? It meant that even though she was playing hard to get, her magic already accepted him.

That made his wolf a little smug.

They pulled up to a brand-new double-wide trailer, the land around it cleared for its placement. Beyond the dirt were piles of sod where it looked like the occupant was getting ready to lay down their lawn. He was glad he'd worn his old boots.

A beautiful woman walked out of the trailer, nearly identical to his mate. Her petite body was stacked, her beautiful face alluring and unlined at her age. He saw where Ness got her dark almond-shaped eyes and full lips. She wore a simple pair of jeans molded to her curves and a plain t-shirt. He couldn't help but smile at the hint of how Ness would age. Her magic was weaving around her in a tight cloud. Trey's wolf perked up, as always interested in power.

Everyone in town knew about Dawn Fouche's drug addiction, but from the bright and clear look on her face, that was in her past. He could respect the work it probably had taken for her to break the vicious habit. In his line of work, he'd seen addiction, and his heart ached for what the witch and his mate may have gone through. While his mother would never outright say anything despairing about the woman, Patrice had added Dawn's drug use as another one of the reasons she didn't want Ness for him. He wouldn't judge Dawn on her past mistakes and looked forward to getting to know Ness's mother as she was now — and not only to gain insight into his mate. She would be a part of his family now, and his uncles had taught him that taking care of family was the mark of a decent man.

Dante grabbed a pair of work gloves and stepped out of the truck. "Mama Dawn," he greeted.

She smiled. "Hey, my baby." She pulled Dante into a hug when he reached the front step.

"Mama, this is my cousin Trey," he introduced.

She smiled warmly. "You one of Patrice's, ain't it?" She squinted and put her hands on her hips. "Which one?"

"The oldest," he answered.

Her face lit up, and she pursed her lips. "Okay, yeah. Interesting. Come in. I got some coffee on for y'all."

They entered her home. The environment was warm and welcoming. He was fascinated with the paintings already on the walls, especially since there were still boxes unopened all around. It seemed she valued the art above all else.

"Sit down, you two. You want something to eat? My daughter brought me pastries yesterday."

"Oh, I'm with that." Dante rubbed his hands together and sat at the small kitchen table behind the sofa delineating the living room from the kitchen.

"Thank you," Trey told her.

Her smile was more mischievous. "So polite. Did you come over here so I'll intervene on your behalf with my daughter?"

He laughed with her. "No, ma'am. I'm making myself known to you because I'm serious about Ness. You'll be a part of my family, and I always take care of mine."

Her eyes lit with pleasure as she lifted the lid off the cake pan full of cinnamon rolls. "Smooth talker."

"Just the truth."

Dante snickered. "This guy."

"We'll see, won't we?" She handed him a small plate and a steaming mug of coffee. "You know your mama don't like Fouches."

He would never allow that to get between him and Ness. "I'll handle my mama."

She snorted but studied him as she sat at the table with them. She propped her chin in her hand. "My daughter may not say it out of her mouth, but Vanessa is looking for a traditional type of family. She didn't have it growing up."

He nodded. "I can give her that and more."

"I want grandbabies."

Dante choked on his coffee, and she snickered.

He wasn't at all intimidated by that. "I'll see what I can do. Your daughter's pretty stubborn."

Dawn outright laughed. "She come by it honestly. Got a temper to match."

"I can handle that, too," he answered.

He felt the probe of her magic. His wolf bristled slightly before settling in for the curious witch. He left himself open, needing her to understand that he had nothing to hide from her or her daughter.

She nodded. "Okay. I like you, Joseph Taylor the Third."

Trey realized that the woman had known exactly who he was before the introductions. He wondered if it was because Ness had talked about him or because the town was so small. It didn't matter either way. He got her approval, and that was all he needed for now.

Hours later, as Trey stepped from his shower, he winced at his tight muscles. He would pay for the manual labor later. It wasn't like he didn't work out, but yardwork used different muscles. All in all, the day was well spent. He got to hang out with his cousin and really liked Ms. Dawn. She was warm and open with him. She'd even given him tips to get through to her daughter as she kissed him on the cheek, and wished him luck. He fingered the small crystal on the end of the black leather necklace she'd bade him to wear on his way out. He couldn't help the smile that tilted his lips as he remembered.

He was slipping into some joggers when the chimes of his security system sounded. It meant someone had entered his property. He lifted his nose and relaxed as he scented JT and his mate and headed toward the door. They were waiting on the porch by the time he reached it. Nic's hand was poised to knock. He stepped back to let them in, kissing the top of Nicole's head as she passed.

"Hi, Trey. I came to check on your tattoos." She threw her thumb over her shoulder. "He's here to make sure your body doesn't get me all hot and bothered."

JT sucked his teeth. "You sure you wanna mess with a Fouche, cuz? All of 'em got a slick mouth."

"You like my mouth," Nic taunted, setting up on Trey's kitchen table.

JT gave her a lascivious look that had Trey rolling his eyes.

"Sit," Nic ordered him.

She pulled out a roll of papers filled with runes and spells. The pages were worn and filled with smeared ink and pencil markings, some of the writing scribbled out and written over. She'd been working on the spells with him for months. Trey had found it all fascinating, but he knew next to nothing about magic, so he'd left it all up to Nic. Typically, a wolf trusting a witch to work magic on them wouldn't happen, but the Fouches and Taylors had worked together for so long that he hadn't given it a second thought.

Nicole used his body as a canvas to prepare him for his relationship with Ness, and he allowed it.

Some part of him should've questioned what the protection was against, but he'd seen how serious Nicole was, and her worry had been conveyed all in her eyes and the animal she was still learning to control. He'd gone with his instincts and allowed it. If it would give her cousin peace of mind, then it would likely do the same for Ness. He'd heard about their family curse and the abysmal outcome for any males involved with the Fouches. The curse had been broken, but as far as he was concerned, between the Taylors' business and his job, he'd never turn down extra protection. He slid out of his tank top so she could examine her work.

Nicole walked behind him and held up the paper. "Did you give them the stuff to add to the ink?"

He nodded. "I went to JT's artist. He already knew the drill."

She hummed. "He did an amazing job," she commented as she came around to check the front. She gasped, and her eyes softened when she saw his chest. "Oh, Trey," she said softly.

Her hand reached out to touch the tattoo on his chest. It was Vanessa's name in delicate script within the handle of a key. The runes that Nicole had him tattoo on his body surrounded it. He figured if the runes meant safety for him, encircling her name with them wouldn't hurt.

"That's honestly the most romantic shit I've ever seen."

"Simp shit," JT muttered as he ate the grapes he'd found in Trey's fridge.

"I know your ass ain't talking," Trey laughed.

"Jeremiah has an overabundance of audacity," Nic said as she examined the rest of the tattoo. She held her hand over it. "I can feel the power, so it's locked and working."

Trey nodded. His wolf had felt the difference the moment the artist had drawn the last line. The whole process had been weird and put his wolf on alert at times, but he was now used to the hum of magic flowing through his bloodstream.

"Have you told Ness?" he asked.

She shook her head. "I'm just following Grandmother's instructions, and according to Patsy, it ain't none of Ness's business. Even though the curse is gone, Grandmother insisted, and I'm not one to disobey her."

"That's so wild to me," he said aloud. That the women could still speak with their grandmother was some powerful shit.

"Has Ness told you what's been going on with her?" Nic asked.

He frowned and thought about the images. They wouldn't leave his head. He debated bringing it up to her cousin, but he didn't want to break Ness's confidence, even if she technically hadn't confided in him.

"What's been happening?" he hedged.

"That's just it. She's not telling us either, but something has been weighing on her. Can you check?"

"Check how, Nic? My baby runs the moment I get too close. You think she gon' talk to me?"

"Could she be in legal trouble?" JT asked.

They both turned their gazes to him.

His cousin shrugged. "Don't be acting like Ness don't be out in these streets wildin'. I'll ask around with some of my connects."

Nic sighed. "Maybe. I'll talk to Bev and see."

He put his shirt back on. "I'll check to see if there are any warrants out on her."

It could be something as simple as that, but he didn't think so. She seemed heavy when he saw her at the bar. He walked them to the door, promising to check in on Ness. He sighed and wiped a hand down his face. What in the world had his mate got herself into?

Chapter Six

To say her relationship with her mother had been tumultuous would be an understatement of epic proportions. In Audrey's case, she'd had to drag her mother out of bars, but there had been no such place for Ness. When Dawn had been in the throes of her drug addiction, a bar would've been the nicest place she could've found her mother.

If Dawn wanted to be found, that is.

There were days, sometimes whole weeks when the woman would disappear, and no amount of searching would lead her only daughter to her. Sometimes, the shame of that would lock Ness in their old trailer, ashamed to even tell her family that Dawn had left her alone. Only when the utilities were cut would Ness finally tell her grandmother. And even during those times, she would try and stick it out for a few days. She hated her grandmother's disappointed and worried look when Ness explained that Dawn was missing once again.

According to the therapy the two of them had been attending together, some of Ness's temper came from a place of resentment for that time. They were working on it, and days like this were the result

of that hard work. Ness walked through the path from her house —
and God, that felt good to say — to Dawn's new trailer. It sat in the
same place as the old one...

That was a trigger she'd examine later.

For now, she kept her steps purposeful. She smiled at the lawn
Dawn had laid out and the small flower garden she saw. Her mother
wasn't much of a gardener, but it meant much to Ness that she would
try. If nothing else, that small patch of dirt proclaimed Dawn's intent
to stay better than her words would have. A pile of lumber to the side
of the steps probably meant Dawn was getting a porch built. That
was good, too. Her mother was putting her inheritance to use, and
with their new relationship, Dawn being around was a good thing.
She still worried about triggers, but Dawn was doing well so far.

She knocked on the door, and her mother answered, a broad
smile on her face. "Baby girl!"

"Hey, mama. I like the new place," Ness greeted.

"I'm still doing work, but it's coming along. I probably should've
built a house, but you know the way my patience is set up."

Ness snorted. "I didn't say anything, mama. It looks nice."

Dawn nodded and moved from the door for her to enter. Before
Ness could step across the threshold, her mother wagged her finger.
"Aht-aht, my daughter enters this space alone."

Dawn pointed to the rune etched into the side of her door near
the doorbell. Ness chuckled and entered her mother's house, happy
for some peace. She shed the spirits she'd been carrying for months,
the rune barring their entry into her mother's space.

"What I tell you about going so long without cleansing, Vanessa?" Dawn asked on her way to the kitchen.

"I know, mama. I just been distracted."

Dawn smirked and gathered her herbs. "I can guess at your
distraction."

Ness looked around, noting her mother's art already hanging on
the wall. She didn't recognize many of the pieces, which was a good

sign. It meant her mother was painting again. Her gaze skimmed over Dawn's hands, noting the flecks of paint. It made her heart smile.

"Speaking of…"

"Were we?" Ness muttered.

"My baby came by here the other day to check on me and brought a cousin of his," Dawn went on.

Ness sucked her teeth and narrowed her eyes at her mother. Dawn unscrewed the cap of a purified water bottle and gave Ness a smug look.

Damn her curiosity. "The hell Dante want?"

"Watch your mouth, lil' girl." Dawn pursed her lips.

Ness knew that look on her mother's face. She was finna pry.

"Him and Joseph came to see if I needed anything."

Dawn's eyes darted over her, searching for answers to the questions she would eventually ask if her daughter missed the hint. Ness's stomach clenched, and she bit her tongue to stop from falling into her mother's baited trap.

Dawn huffed. "I know you and Dante ain't meant for each other, but he turned into such a good man and will always be my baby. That Joseph will make a good son-in-law, though."

Lord have mercy.

Ness stayed silent, watching as her mother prepared the herb bath for her cleansing. She refused to lift her eyes from the glass bowl.

Dawn continued. "He was very polite, and all that power… You got a good one in him. I know Patrice fixin' to lose her shit now that her son is mating with a Fouche. I wish I could see her sanctified face."

Ness barely kept from rolling her eyes, but Dawn seemed to sense it and laughed. She bowed her head with her mother as she prayed over the bowl of herbs and water. Ness watched her as she walked out the back door. Dawn returned empty-handed, leaving the herbs in the sun to power.

"Now that that's out of the way, tell me about you and Trey. What's going on there?"

"There's nothing going on," she muttered.

Dawn's lips twitched, but she held back her smile. "You know, when Israel told us that we would all have to keep our cats, I was a little scared and skeptical. For so long, I'd been wrestling with its power. But now, having full use of all these extra senses is something else. Would you agree?"

The 'cat' her mother referenced being stuck with was a part of a curse that had been placed on their family. Months ago, with Israel's help, they'd been able to break the curse, but doing so had meant keeping the puma spirit a part of them. Unlike natural born shifters, the Fouche women were only able to shift during the full moon, but the sharpened senses that came with the animal spirit was with them permanently. So, she knew exactly what her mother meant...but she wouldn't give Dawn the satisfaction.

Ness only narrowed her eyes, waiting for her mother's point.

"I mean, I could already tell when you were lying, but it's interestin' to have confirmation from this animal."

"Get to the point, Dawn Fouche," she huffed out.

Her mother gave her a megawatt smile, knowing she'd successfully gotten under Ness's skin. "I ain't gon' say nothing else. Except... I recognized his scent as having been all over Mama's property." Dawn tapped her nose. "Extra senses and all."

Ness stiffened her shoulders. True to Dawn's word, she didn't elaborate.

"You ate yet, baby girl?"

Ness shook her head, a little disoriented.

"Well, I don't cook like you, but I guess I can throw something on the stove so we can have a meal together." Dawn led them to the sofa in her living room.

"It's two in the afternoon, mama. I ain't trying to eat at no early bird special ass time."

Dawn reached over and thumped her hand. "That smart-ass mouth of yours. Fine. We'll sit on the sofa and starve to death."

Ness snorted at that exaggeration.

"I got a movie I saved on Lifetime for us to watch anyways."

Ness smiled, grabbed the blanket her mother kept on the sofa, and leaned her head on Dawn's shoulder. She could get in the mood for a corny movie.

"You feel whole," she commented, taking in her mother's presence.

"My nephew finished the work Mama started."

Ness sat up. "Israel did?"

At her mother's nod, she settled her head back. She would make sure to thank her new cousin. Having her mother healthy and sane was a gift she wouldn't take for granted. She'd known that coming home would unearth a lot of the trauma her family had faced, but Ness had been so shocked at the skeletons that had come tumbling from the Fouches' closets.

She'd thought her mother's drug use had been the result of Dawn being unable to handle the power that ran in her family. It turned out to be the result of a ritual that had gone wrong when her aunt Kit had tried to resurrect her mate from the dead. Using dark magic with her sister's help, they had tried swapping a homeless person's soul with that of Kit's husband. The karmic backlash had sent both women spiraling into substance abuse for years.

Even as powerful as Patsy had been, she'd been unable to help her daughters. That Audrey's husband Israel had been able to pick up where their grandmother left off was a godsend.

"That boy got a lot of power. You girls chose well."

Ness rolled her eyes at her mother, circling back. "I don't have a man," she muttered.

"My son-in-law laid down my grass and helped Dante clear me an area for my garden, so you can lie to yourself, but I'm claiming him."

Ness snickered at the ridiculous woman. It was useless to even argue with Dawn Fouche. Her mother kissed the top of her head and started the movie. Ness could only give thanks that the two of them had arrived at this place. It had been a hard road. Her body stiffened as she looked at the painting above her mother's television. It depicted the woods that surrounded all their houses. Fire blazed across the canvas in bold, fiery strokes. Her mother was so talented that it took her breath away. Ness shivered at the darkness in stark contrast with the blaze in the woods. She understood the ominous undertone.

"When did you paint that?" She fought to keep her voice calm.

"A year ago. That painting is what convinced me to come home when Shelby called," Dawn answered, kissing the top of Ness's head. "That's a worry for another day, my love."

Ness forced her body to relax, but her eyes kept straying to the painting. She prayed she would be able to keep her family safe.

Ness would never admit aloud to the nervousness circling her gut as she sat in her car, staring at Trey's one-story house. The yard was well-kept and homey. It made her think he would be a good family man. Or maybe Dawn's words had her looking at him differently. She sighed and shook her head. That's not why she was here. She was going to thank him for helping her mother, and that was it. She'd done the same for Dante, taking him over his favorite dessert.

This was no different.

Trey was no different than her relationship with any of the other Taylors.

Her grandmother scoffed. *"Tell yourself anything, chile."*

Ness sighed again. Her mother's cleansing had rid her of all of the spirits that had clung to her aura for the past few months, but there was no getting rid of Patsy. Candace had kept herself quiet, but

Ness could feel her too, just on the edge of her consciousness. As the woman had told her many times, she was her appointed guide and was there to stay.

Ignoring her grandmother, she grabbed the cake from her passenger seat and left the car. Her heart was thundering as she got closer, her steps slow as she ascended his front porch. She rang the doorbell with a shaking hand.

Trey opened the door with a smile on his face. He wore a black sleeveless shirt with loose pants in the same color. The pants were thin enough to outline the shape of his—

She snatched her eyes back up to his face, her cheeks hot. "I... umm..."

"Brought me cake," he finished for her, a mischievous smile on his face. "Come in, baby girl."

He backed away from the door to give her room to enter. Though she didn't plan to stay long, she wanted privacy with him, so she pulled chalk from her pocket. "Is it okay if I..." she trailed off.

He pointed at the rune under the sconce on his wall. "Already done."

She wanted to ask if that was for her benefit but wasn't ready for the answer, so she entered. It, however, reminded her of Dawn's point about Trey's scent all over her grandmother's house. She'd tested it for herself when she left her mother's. The man had scent-marked the whole yard. While she was struggling with...whatever this could be between them, it seemed Trey was getting prepared for it.

"Nice place," she said as she entered.

"Thanks, my mama did it. It's supposed to be temporary in case my mate wants to live someplace else."

This man. She took a deep breath and fought to control her heart rate. She'd known that Trey was charming. Even from observing him afar, he had a way with people. But she hadn't been prepared for the full scale of his charisma when it was aimed her way. The man was kind of irresistible. If she was smart, she'd leave while she was ahead. It was only a matter of time before she caved in to him.

She cleared her throat. "Where can I put this?"

He watched her, his heated gaze sending goosebumps across her skin. He nodded toward the kitchen. She walked over to the small dining table and set the cake down, taking a shaky breath.

"It's carrot."

"My favorite," he said with a smile that made her wet.

"I wanted to thank you for helping my mom."

Now that her hands were empty, she was at a loss. She clutched them tightly in front of her lest she be tempted to touch his arms. He walked up to her and closed the distance between them.

"I see where you got all that gorgeousness from."

She snorted. "Don't be trying to game me, Joseph."

He laughed. "Always calling me by my full government name."

"It's your name." She bit her lip to keep from smiling because, despite her words, she was definitely falling for his game.

"Along with two others in the family."

Her smile won, tilting her lips. "Is that why they call you Trey?"

"Uno, dos, Trey," he counted on his fingers.

She laughed. "I'm pretty sure that's not how that went."

He shrugged, his teasing smile infectious. "What you doing tonight?"

"Trey."

He stepped into her space. "Let's have dinner together. I'll even cook."

"Can you cook?"

He slid his arm around her waist and inhaled, his eyes closing. "Only one way to find out, kitty cat."

She studied the hard planes of his face, debating it. He was so damn fine. Despite the trouble she'd bring to his door, every ounce of her wanted him. Hadn't she earned herself a little grace? She hadn't been arrested in years and was now on the straight and narrow, thanks to her inheritance. Her cousins were all settling down, wasn't it time for her to do the same? Couldn't she just see what things could be like with Trey?

Though her grandmother wasn't in her ear at the moment, she could hear Patsy's encouragement. Perhaps it was her mother's words to her that added to the temptation. Nothing had changed, really. She still had a bounty on her head and a warlock that would likely show up in town any day now and cause havoc, so she should be preparing for that.

But...

It was just dinner.

She nodded, and her stomach fluttered when he nuzzled against her cheek. She could feel the power of his animal enveloping her in a cocoon of safety. If she sat with it long enough, she'd realize that even with their banter, she'd always felt that way with Trey. But that was for later. She'd examine that when she was alone.

"I'm gonna be on my best behavior, I promise," he murmured against her skin.

His words sent heat straight to her torso, clenching her stomach. What did his best behavior look like?

Chapter Seven

As he served them dinner, Trey realized Ness was the first woman he'd cooked for. He followed his animal in everything, so getting serious with a woman other than his mate had never been an option. He'd dated casually, yes, but he'd never put forth the effort required to nourish a relationship. It was a novel experience, cooking for his mate.

Her eyes lit with pleasure when he placed the bowl of shrimp and grits in front of her. It was one of his favorite meals and easy to cook on short notice.

She leaned down and inhaled. "I'm impressed."

It warmed his heart. He sat across from her, grabbing her hands to say grace. They were quiet for a few minutes as they ate. He was pleased to have her in his house, eating from his hand, so he was content.

"My mama likes you." She broke the silence a few minutes later.

He laughed. "Your mom is good people."

"Was her interrogation subtle?"

"Not even a little bit," he admitted.

It was her turn to laugh. He loved seeing her happy. He could see the heaviness her cousins were worried about. It dimmed the natural light of her eyes. She was full of secrets, his mate, but he would work on getting her comfortable enough to share them with him.

"Do you like being sheriff?" she asked.

Trey shrugged. "It's a job. It helps me keep my cousins out of too much trouble, and it keeps my mother from worrying I'm headed to hell."

Ness snickered. "I've talked to your little brother before, but up until a few years ago, I'd never run into you."

"I still remember my first glimpse of you," he mused.

She lifted her wine glass but said nothing, only inclining her head for him to continue. He paused a beat, unsure how much he wanted to tell her. Not that any of it was secret, but suddenly, he felt vulnerable. Goosebumps erupted on his arms as he thought of the first hint of her scent that had reached him. Trey had paused mid-stride to trace it. She'd been at the front desk, a smug smile on her beautiful face as the deputy had been forced to uncuff her.

Her hair had been in locs, wild and flowing down her back, and her body...good God. She wore a baggy t-shirt tied above her navel and a pair of biker shorts that showcased her curvy ass. He was embarrassed to tell her he'd damn near gone to his knees. Her gorgeous face was bare, though her full, pouty lips were glossy. The thick lashes that framed her dark eyes made her look like a doll.

Everything about the woman had spelled trouble, and his wolf wanted all parts of it.

"From the moment your scent drifted to me, I knew you were mine," he said instead of all that.

She sucked in a sharp breath. "Why didn't you say anything then?"

Again, he tempered his words. He'd finally gotten her to agree to dinner; he had no intention of scaring her off. But then...he decided to throw caution to the wind. Perhaps the secret was assuring her of his intentions.

"I'm the kind of person that likes to plan. I don't move until I'm sure of my footing. You...you're ethereal, almost otherworldly in your beauty and the power surrounding you. I knew catching you could maybe be easy, but I didn't want to just catch you. I want to keep you. That's a whole separate game requiring a more...careful set of rules. You understand what I mean?"

She swallowed and nodded, her body tense, the skittish part of her probably counting the steps to the front door. He grabbed her hand gently.

"I had to get my shit in order so that when I caught you, I was ready for you." He twined their fingers together, his thumb brushing her skin lightly. "And now that I'm secure, I can be whatever you need. My world is stable, rock-solid, so no matter what you're going through, I'll be steady for you."

Ness turned her head, but not before he saw the moisture gathering in her eyes. He released her hand and allowed her a few moments of peace, knowing what he'd laid on her was heavy. He collected their dishes and dropped them into the sink. By the time he turned around with smaller plates for the cake, she'd gathered herself together.

"You want more wine?"

She shook her head. "I got more baking to do when I get home."

"What are you making?"

"Audrey and Dame are doing this kind of happy hour thing at the brewery now. It's a tasting, but I make these little mini cakes and things to accompany each one." Her eyes lit up when she started talking about it.

He cut them both a slice and asked her more about her family's microbrewery. He knew that their grandmother had left it to the three cousins in her will. So far, Ness and Audrey seemed more involved in the day-to-day than Nic. With the conversation lighter, Ness relaxed, and they were able to talk comfortably. Before he knew it, hours had passed.

Ness set her glass of water down and clasped her hands together. "I should go," she said softly.

"You drove?" he asked, standing with her.

She nodded, and he walked her to the door.

"The cake was amazing and very much appreciated. If you need someone to taste test, I'm your guy."

She laughed. "I'll keep that in mind."

He stood at the door, his shoulder against the jamb. He pulled her into his arms before she got too far away from him.

Trey slid a finger down her cheek before dropping a small kiss on her lips. "Text me when you get home."

"You're not going to try and convince me to stay?" She cocked her head and studied him.

He gripped the back of her neck and scraped his teeth down her skin. His wolf bucked within his body, urging him to push for more.

"Your actions say you not ready, kitty cat."

He smiled as the cat inside of her flashed in irritation, her skin heating beneath his hand. Oh, his mate hated being told no. He noted it for later. The power this woman put off would burn him and his wolf to a cinder, and he was looking forward to it. She stepped out of his arms, her hands shaky as she straightened her dress. She looked at him again. This time, her confusion was perfectly under-standable.

She was probably used to leading men around by the leash.

He would probably be the same way, but not until she was his. He had no desire for her to discard him like she may have done the others before him. He wasn't worried about any man she'd had in her life before him.

He knew that he would be the last.

She turned to walk away, but he stopped her, tipping her chin up so that he could stare into her eyes.

"That doesn't mean you can't call me if you need anything. No matter what it is, baby girl. No judgment."

He held her gaze until she dipped her head in agreement. He wanted to be the person she went to when she needed something. He understood how close she was to his cousins, but he'd already told them that he was the one she would be calling from now on. She was his, and nothing would change that.

Her eyes flickered to the side before settling back on him. "I'll remember that."

He kissed her forehead. "Alright, then. Good night, Vanessa."

"Good night, Joseph."

He let her go with a smirk. His wolf was kicking his ass about it. He stood at the door until she drove down his driveway and her brake lights disappeared into the night. He thought briefly of changing into his wolf form and following her home, but that reached stalker territory, and he wasn't sure he wanted to show that side of himself. He'd already allowed his wolf to leave his mark on her property. He was probably pushing way past his mate's comfort zone.

She may not have been ready for him yet, but it wouldn't stop him and his wolf from letting the rest of the world know that she belonged to them.

One convenient thing about the sheriff's station being in the middle of Westport was the view from Trey's office. If he leaned just right, he could see the small warehouse that housed Springbrook Microbrewery. Mind, he had to be damn near leaning to the floor in his chair, but the point still stood. Trey's office was in the back of the sheriff's station, so instead of watching the main road and passing traffic, his view consisted of the back of the stores that filled the shopping center.

Most importantly, the employee parking.

It was how he'd spotted his mate as she pulled into the microbrewery the Fouches owned and operated. Trey smiled and stood, rushing from his office. It had been a couple of days since he'd last seen her, and he and his wolf missed her. He grabbed a walkie from the front on his way out to remain within reach. By the time he'd weaved through the back parking lot, Ness was making a second trip to her car. She looked up in surprise as he grabbed the platter from her hand.

"Afternoon, baby girl," Trey muttered, leaning down to kiss her forehead.

"Sheriff," she greeted, a pout gracing her mug.

If she knew what that was doing to his body, she'd likely straighten her face. "Why you mad at me?"

"Ain't nobody thinking about you, Trey," she snapped.

He chuckled, wondering if her attitude with him was over him telling her no. He gently placed the container of cakes on the top of her car and invaded her space. She let out an irritated sigh and looked up at him.

He stepped closer and cupped her chin. "What's the matter?"

She growled, the angry sound surprising him. "Trey, stop trying to fix shit for me."

Now was probably the best time for her to learn that her moodiness wouldn't phase him. He wasn't in the habit of getting riled up easily.

"Baby girl, you gotta use words with me. Pouting and throwing a fit don't do me nothing." He gripped the back of her neck gently.

His wolf rumbled his chest with a growl, sending an entreaty to her cat for submission. The cat conceded, but the woman was still irked.

"Now, what's wrong?"

"I don't want to talk about it," she whispered.

"You mad at me, kitty cat?" He nuzzled the side of her face.

Her breath brushed his skin as she sighed, her body finally relaxing in his arms. She didn't answer.

He studied her but nodded. "I'll let it be for now, then. You need anything?"

"Not like you finna give me what I want anyways," she pouted.

Oh, it was definitely about the other night. He chuckled. "Just because I won't fuck you now don't mean I won't make up for making you wait, kitty cat."

She gasped. "Excuse your damn nerve," she sputtered.

Her magic flared, and the cold lash of it stung his skin as she let her irritation be known. This woman hated being called out. Was it weird that he found her flash of temper adorable? He swallowed his laugh and changed the subject.

"I'm out of cake, baby girl."

"Too damn bad," she muttered.

"Don't do your mate like that, ma." He sucked on her neck, his tongue sliding across her skin. "I want brownies this time."

She sucked her teeth, moving restlessly in his arms. The scent of her arousal rose between them, and Trey could only breathe it in and hold her tight, or he'd lose the tiny bit of control he had over his wolf.

"I'm not your personal baker," she murmured breathlessly.

He hummed, ignoring her protest, slipping his hand underneath the tank she wore. He sighed in pleasure at the feel of her soft skin against his palm. Pressing the small of her back, he brought her closer into him. He knew his erection was poking in her stomach, but there was nothing he could do about that.

"Anyone can see you out here rubbing all up on a Fouche, Sheriff Taylor," she admonished.

He didn't give a fuck. Especially since all the fire in her voice was gone, replaced by a contented purr. He loved that sound and promised himself to provide her with plenty of reasons to use it with him.

"That ain't my business, Vanessa. You are."

Her breath hitched, and she wrapped her arms around his waist. He didn't say anything, just gave her the comfort her cat was asking his wolf for — even as the woman fought him. The cool breeze of her magic wrapped around him, none of the sting from before. Their gazes locked, a gentle meeting that conveyed the feelings they were both holding for each other. Yeah, Ness was running, but her soul belonged with him, and it had no such doubts or confusion. Her magic wove a spell around him until everything in their vicinity dimmed and was replaced by a vision that stole his breath.

He could see their life together.

A lump filled his throat as he observed the image of Ness holding his daughter in her arms, a wide smile on her face. It felt like he could reach out and touch that image. He gripped her tighter, trying to hold onto it. Ness gasped and stepped back.

"Trey," she whispered.

His walkie-talkie squawked at his hip, breaking the tense silence between them. He took a deep, shaky breath before unclipping it.

"Go, baby girl," he murmured, kissing her lightly.

She grabbed the last desserts and headed for the back door of the brewery. He waited until she was safely inside before answering his deputy's summons.

"Yeah?"

"Got a witch trying to cross the county line over here on 17," his deputy reported.

Trey sighed and headed to his truck. He was off shift in another hour but knew anything could happen between then and now. He drove toward the gas station separating Westport County from the neighboring county, knowing he'd stationed a deputy there earlier. He made it there in record time, the image of him and Ness's children playing in his head.

Fuck, he wanted that more than anything.

He shook the image away for now, needing to focus on work. When he arrived, he stepped out of the truck, narrowing his eyes on the tall Asian woman standing between his two deputies. She was young in initial appearance, but it certainly was no indication of her power. He could feel that from across the parking lot.

She straightened her shoulders as he approached. "Your deputies are harassing me. They can't keep me from entering your little piece-of-shit town. That's discrimination."

Trey paused her rant by holding up his hand. "Not many people know this, but a few of our deputies are magic users."

Her eyes widened, and her chest deflated.

"So you see, had you simply been trying to travel through town, there would've been no problem. I assume that if they stopped you, you were doing some kind of illegal magic. Is that right, deputy?"

Oliver Thomas was a warlock and new to the force but slowly growing confident in his job. "She was driving through using a locator spell."

"That's very illegal." Trey crossed his arms over his chest.

It was one of the first spells made illegal when magic users had come out of hiding. It had only taken a few dozen witnesses lost to the US Marshalls before the legislature had been written.

"I'm looking for my friend."

"Funny. The cell service in this town works just fine," Trey said dryly. "Who's your friend?"

"Am I being arrested?" she asked instead of answering his question.

"I can see myself convinced to leave it at a ticket if you go on about your business," he told her.

His wolf didn't like her one bit. Trey inhaled deeply to take in her scent. He would commit it to memory.

"Fine," she huffed out, and Trey nodded to his deputy.

He returned to his SUV and leaned against the front while watching them give the witch a ticket. They looked at him, and he inclined his head. They followed the woman as she pulled out of the gas station and would stay behind her until she crossed the lines that ended their jurisdiction. He wondered who she was trying to locate.

Time would tell if she'd become a problem. Besides, he had better things to think about. Namely, how to get the vision of his mate and children to come true.

Chapter Eight

She was making brownies.

Damn that man.

Ness could only shake her head in defeat as she and her little cousin spread batter into the pans they'd greased earlier. She was trying to be mad at him, but it was really useless, not to mention petty. How was she going to be mad at him for not sleeping with her when she kept telling him that she wasn't checking for him?

Pathetic.

She was baking for a man who wouldn't even dick her down.

"Your cake should be ready," she clumsily signed to her little cousin.

Brina smiled wide and rushed to the oven to look. They'd been baking all morning. Ness had been surprised when the young girl had knocked on her door and volunteered to help bake the birthday cake Ness was making for her father. She was supposed to be at her grandmother's helping to decorate for the dinner they were having tonight, but Shelby had given her the okay. Brina was a sweet girl, and despite Ness's sign language being rudimentary at best, the two had gotten along swimmingly.

"It looks good!" Brina signed, dancing in place.

Ness laughed and pulled it from the oven. She slid the brownies in its place and let out a sigh. What was it about Trey? He was charming, she'd give him that, but it was something else. The cat inside her moved through her body restlessly, and Ness shook her head. The animal knew what it was, but the woman still held on to her denial. The closer to the full moon, the more the puma made its presence and needs known. And it wanted Trey.

Her phone vibrated across the kitchen counter, and her heart thudded. She snatched it up and turned her back to Brina to keep her from being able to read her lips. She answered despite the blocked number. Hiding seemed useless at this point.

"Yes?"

"Meet with me."

The voice wasn't who she was expecting, and while that gave her a slight reprieve, she was still shaken. Monica was a private detective she'd worked with before on her insurance fraud cases. The witch was exceptional at her job, so the company she'd worked for kept her on retainer. If Monica had already found her, then that meant Zane wasn't far behind. She took a shaky breath and brushed a hand over her hair, steadying her nerves.

"We don't have any reason to meet."

Monica sighed. "You know as well as I do that meeting with me is the safest thing you can do right now, Vanessa Fouche."

Ness's pulse sped. It had taken them a year to find out her real name, but with that came a plethora of information. It was only a matter of time before they found her family. Zane and his organization were notorious for the many ways they got people to cooperate. Going after their families was the main one.

Fuck.

She couldn't lead them here. "I'll send you an address."

There was one place where she could meet with Monica away from Fouche land where she would be protected. That would mean possibly having to talk to Audrey, and that was risky. She and her cousin were close enough that Audrey would ask questions. But what was her alternative? Meet Monica here? Out of the question.

"Tomorrow morning. This is your last chance before he comes down himself," Monica threatened before ending the call.

Ness jumped as she felt the tap on her shoulder. She turned and faced Brina's concerned face.

"Is everything okay?" Brina signed.

Ness nodded. "Fine," she said aloud.

Marcellus walked through the back door before Brina could pry further, and Ness breathed a sigh of relief. She needed to be alone to think and plan. Her cousin studied her as he came in.

"It smells amazing in here," he said and signed. "Brina, your mother is waiting at the house for you."

"I made you a cheesecake," Brina informed him.

Cellus smiled and pulled his daughter in for a hug. Ness found it hard to swallow as emotions filled her. Her cousins were doing so well. She couldn't let her shit fall back onto them. She turned away from the beautiful picture they made and cleaned up the kitchen. She heard the back door open and close but felt Cellus's presence.

"Now, what's wrong?"

She blew out a breath and turned to face her oldest cousin. Marcellus had long ago deemed himself their protector and took his role seriously.

"It's nothing I can't handle," she answered.

"Baby girl..." he started.

She held up her hand. "It's my mess to clean up, Cellus, and I'll clean it up in my own time."

"If you talking like that, I already know Nic has no idea."

That was true, though she didn't know how long it would take before Nicole took matters into her own hands. Nic didn't pry, but she also didn't like problems lingering. She was a head-on type of person.

She shrugged.

"Do I need to give my wife a heads up?" He smiled.

"I am not in legal trouble," she stressed.

She only wished it were as simple as that. Hell, she'd gladly take a court case over a powerful warlock being after her. She knew eventually she'd have to tell everyone, but that time wasn't now. Cellus watched her with his arms crossed over his chest. It was written all over his face that he wanted to ask more questions, but he dropped it with a sigh.

"Mama said you and the sheriff were dating. Is that true?" Cellus asked, grabbing a cookie from the jar she kept in the middle of the island.

Lord have mercy. If he was asking, then that meant gossip was all over town. She wanted to deny it, but the words wouldn't come. Instead, she told her cousin, "None of your business."

"That means yes." He laughed. "You must be *done* done with crime-ing, then."

She busted out laughing. "Don't do me. I ain't been arrested in years."

"All that tells me is that you haven't been caught," he joked.

He had no idea how true that was. "That cheesecake needs to go in the fridge before y'all eat it."

"Changing the subject? Oh, you guilty." He chuckled and lifted the warm cake.

"You can go now," she told him, holding the back door open.

He kissed the top of her head as he passed. "I ain't the only one noticing your mood, baby girl. It would be best to say something soon before they pull an intervention. You coming by Mama's tonight?"

"I might stop through for a little bit. I don't even like you like that."

Cellus chortled. "If you don't show up, I may start instigating."

Now, see... "You get on my nerves."

He gave her a two-finger salute and headed toward the path to his mother's house. She closed the door and locked it. She knew that Cellus was right. So far, her family had allowed her to put off their questions, but she had a feeling that wouldn't last too much longer.

Even knowing how her cousins would feel about it, Ness got on the road to the meeting spot the following day. She'd had all night to tell them what was happening, yet she hadn't. For a moment this morning, she'd wavered as she'd gotten dressed, but in the end, she'd rather risk her safety than theirs. There was no way to predict the direction of the meeting, and she had a feeling that if she had told Nic or Audrey that she was headed to Savannah, one or both of them would've been in the car beside her.

"But no. All you have is us," Patsy said next to her.

Ness sighed. Yes. She was headed to meet a powerful witch armed only with two guide spirits.

"Not that we are useless," Candace piped up from the back.

"I didn't say that," Ness muttered.

"Who is the witch?" Patsy asked.

"Someone I used to work with," she answered.

"At which job? The one you did on paper, or the one where you and Candace were stealing family heirlooms?"

The way her grandmother said it, it clearly wasn't a question. So, Ness didn't bother answering it. No one had known about her side gig, and had she not made this last mistake, that would still hold true. Cellus had only suspicions regarding her work but no hard proof. She'd worked hard to keep her last identity squeaky clean. She'd liked the work she did for the insurance company, having lucked into the appraiser job. Her faked credentials had gotten her in the door, but her magic had pushed her to the top of the field.

She didn't imagine other appraisers could read the old objects to assess their value. For once, the magic she'd been born with had helped in her legal work. Her side business had been born when one of the spirits attached to an object had begged her to return it to its rightful owners.

Her grandmother saw it as stealing, and...yes, technically, it was. She stole stuff, but only from the people they didn't belong to. Her side job hit that sweet spot of legally wrong but morally right. And as far as she was concerned, it assuaged her sense of justice, so she'd never had an issue with it. Plus, in some — most — instances, it paid well. The tips she received from some of the families paid for the lavish lifestyle she used to lead. She thought she'd miss it, but being home with her cousins was dredging up some of the dreams she used to have for herself. And none of them had a thing to do with material items.

There was one man in particular who had her thinking about those daydreams.

Sheriff: *Thank you for my brownies, baby girl.*

Speak of the devil.

She'd dropped off his brownies at the sheriff's office this morning before she'd left town. She was lucky that he'd been out. The temptation to confide in him, to ask his advice, was too much. Had she seen him, she would've spilled it all. His daily text messages were starting to make her feel like they were in a relationship already. He'd told Ness he would be a steady place for her, and the thought of that appealed to her more and more every day.

He made her feel safe. For someone who'd been solo dolo for so long, it was a foreign feeling but not unwelcome. She and her cousins were getting back to the close relationships they had as kids, so she wasn't alone anymore. But habits were hard to break, and confiding in another person was even more challenging.

Sheriff: *Call me when you get a chance.*

Despite the worry about her meeting, she smiled. He had that effect on her. She couldn't respond while she was on the interstate, but she'd make sure to answer him later because the last thing she needed was him hunting her down and finding out she'd left town.

Thirty minutes later, she pulled into the restaurant's parking lot where she'd arranged the meeting with Monica. She sent a quick message to Nicole and Audrey as a 'just in case' and shoved her phone into her purse. Taking a deep breath, she got out.

The small café was busy, but she immediately spotted Monica at a table outside on their patio. The witch was tall and graceful. From the no-nonsense braid trailing her shoulder to the simple jeans and polo, everything about Monica showcased her practical nature. In the grand scheme of things, she was the better alternative. Taking a careful look around before she sat, Ness was confident that no one else was waiting to ambush her.

"With the last number I saw for the bounty on your head, I'm surprised you showed up," Monica greeted.

It had given Ness pause, for sure. Being out in public was risky, but she was out of options. At least until she told her cousins.

"Let's get this over with."

"You look good for someone on the run from the government," Monica said as she studied her.

"Zane is hardly the whole government," Ness said flippantly. She refused to let on how worried she actually was.

Monica shrugged. "All the same. He's not someone you can cross and then walk away from."

"What does he want?" She needed to cut through all the small talk and get to the heart of it.

In the best-case scenario, Zane would ask her to steal back what she'd taken from him or to steal something of equal value. She wouldn't be opposed to the latter option, but stealing the cross back would be complicated.

"He wants what you stole from him, but more than that, he wants to make an example out of you," Monica said bluntly.

She had no skin in the game on either side. It was one of Monica's most sought-after qualities. She got paid to do a job and did it well without prying into her clients' affairs.

"You and I know I can't steal back a holy relic from the fucking Vatican," Ness snapped, irritated with the whole thing.

Monica shrugged. "I don't even know what it is. That's not my business. My business was finding you and relaying my client's wishes."

"So what's the rest?"

Monica studied her before answering. "You're usually a lot more discreet."

Ness shifted in surprise. She wasn't expecting that. "You don't say no to the Vatican." But mostly, she couldn't say no to the amount of money they'd offered.

Monica nodded as though that answer made sense. "I thought he would ask for an artifact of equal power, but that's not what he wants."

This was where it would get tricky. Zane was a powerful warlock, but that wasn't what necessarily worried her. She could deal with power. Zane was greedy in his need for control, and that made him ruthless and unreasonable. Plus, he worked for the paranormal department of the federal government. Were it him alone, perhaps she would have a chance. With this, her standard negotiating tactics wouldn't work.

"What does he want?"

"There are rumors about the land your family owns," was all she said.

A chill raced down Ness's spine. Nothing else needed to be said. There were generations of power imbued into her family's land. She could understand why that would be tempting to someone like Zane. Like her, he had some powers of necromancy. She didn't want to know what he would do on her ancestral land.

"Zane can kiss my ass."

Monica pinched her lips. "That's the message you want me to give to him?"

"His terms are unacceptable. You can tell him that however you see fit." Ness crossed her arms over her chest.

"You don't want me to tell him that." Monica sat back in her chair and tossed her braid over her shoulder. "You know as well as I that he won't take that as an answer."

"It's the only answer he's getting. My family land is not up for negotiation."

Ness stood, done with the conversation. She didn't care what it would take. She would fight with her last breath for her family.

Monica slapped down an envelope, and pictures slid out of it across the table. Ness stared at it a moment before giving in to curiosity and reclaiming her seat. She moved the envelope and its contents closer, spreading them out. The cat within her bucked as she viewed pictures of her family members. There were even images of her cousin Julian and his children. Marcellus's brother was in Atlanta and much easier to get to than the rest of them. Ness cursed internally and slid the pictures back inside.

"My answer still stands," she said with a shaky voice.

It was time to tell her family. If it were just herself that they were threatening, she could maybe justify keeping it from them, but this... They would never forgive her if she let them get blindsided.

"He won't give you any other warnings, Olivia." Monica shook her head. "Vanessa, I mean."

Before Ness could say anything, Monica grabbed her own throat, eyes widening in panic. Ness felt the pressure of gathering magic and sent a panicked look around.

She didn't have to look long. Her new cousin-in-law swaggered over to their table. Israel was dressed in all black despite the warm weather. His slacks were custom-tailored and paired with a simple v-neck t-shirt. The man exuded power and money, both things he'd grown up with. His thick dark brows were lowered over his eyes in a menacing glare he leveled at Monica as he continued to cut off her airway with his magic.

It took a moment for Ness to shake off her shock. "It's fine, Israel."

He tilted his head at her in acknowledgment, releasing the witch. He grabbed Monica's arm and moved her from the seat, taking her place as the witch heaved and coughed beside him.

"This is my city, little witch. You don't enter without my permission, and you certainly don't level threats at my family." He leaned his elbows on the table. "Do you know who I am?"

Monica nodded, coughing as air filled her lungs again.

"Run along now."

"He's going to come for you," Monica warned Ness with a wheeze.

"I suggest you find yourself something safe to do, girl, before I get mean," Israel gave his own warning.

Eli, Israel's head enforcer and best friend, walked up behind Monica, releasing a growl. The witch jumped in fear. She held up her hands, grabbed her bag from the back of the chair, and rushed out of the restaurant.

Ness released the breath she'd been holding. "Iz."

"What's going on, cousin-in-law?" He leaned back with his arm thrown over the back of the chair.

"I'm good. What are you doing here?"

"Checking on you. You sent my wife a cryptic message, so here I am."

Ness sighed and repeated, "I'm good."

"Audrey won't accept that answer," he told her.

She was well aware of that, but right now, fear had a knot firmly lodged in her throat. She could easily tell Israel her problem, and he would help her simply because Audrey had asked. Things were serious now.

"Why come way out this way?" he asked.

"I didn't want to lead them to Springbrook." It was an honest answer. Plus, she knew his power and felt safe enough, knowing he was in the city.

Israel hummed. "Okay, I'll let it go for now. Who was the witch?"

"We used to work together. She's a private detective." She kept her answer short.

"She was sent to find you?"

Ness nodded reluctantly.

"Tell your cousins. Soon, Ness. I don't like problems that can pop up."

"I swear," she promised him.

"I'll see you for Sunday dinner, then." With that, he stood, and he and Eli left the restaurant.

Ness took a deep breath and ran a shaking hand down her face. The time for stalling was over. A wave of despair overtook her at the thought of what they would think of her. They often joked that she kept herself in trouble and at times, she laughed along with them, but proving them right had shame roiling in her gut. She'd tried to keep her family out of her illegal activities for the most part. It was one of the reasons Bev and her had grown so close over the years. The woman had kept Ness's secrets.

Ness walked back to her car with shaking legs, the world around her blurry as tears pooled in her eyes. Her cousins would never forgive her for this.

Chapter Nine

Trey was on his third brownie as he sat at the edge of town perusing his laptop, looking through the rap sheet they had on Ness. He eyed the brownies and debated another but decided against it. He was shocked when he arrived at his office and found them with a note from his mate. His mood had been high all day. She still hadn't hit him back when he'd texted her earlier, but that was fine. He had every intention of swinging by her house when he got off.

At the moment, he was sitting in his parked SUV on the edge of Springbrook. He'd been checking out a report about a rogue shifter that had turned out to be a false alarm. He could've returned to the sheriff's office, but he hadn't been in the mood to drive back to town. Calling off and going home was another option, but so was going through the database and running the clock out on his shift. Here in this small cut was as good of a place as any to do the research he wanted. Not a lot of cars passed along the stretch of road in front of him, so he would have privacy among the towering pine trees.

JT had called him earlier with some news that he was still digesting. His wolf was of a mind to chase their mate down and lock her away somewhere safe, but he wanted time to think through his options.

According to his cousin, Ness had a two-million-dollar bounty on her head. He still couldn't process that that amount of money was being offered for the capture of his mate. He'd put his brother on it immediately to track the source. Richie hadn't gotten back to him yet, but Trey knew it would take some time.

He'd taken JT's other advice and looked through the local data-base for her records. He hadn't found anything a few days ago when he looked, but now he was trying the federal one. Getting access was a little trickier, but he'd found a way. Ness had been in a lot of trouble at one time, and he could only sigh— that woman.

Most of her file was filled with petty charges, but as of six years ago, there was nothing else added. What had changed? Not that he'd expected her to have a new file every year, but it was curious that everything had stopped. Ness was clever, he had no doubt about that, but with the amount of power she wielded, he'd expected the feds to keep an eye on her. Instead, there was nothing, no new warrants or any other arrests for her for six years, which was a good thing. It meant she'd been keeping herself out of trouble.

Interesting.

He tapped his fingers against the top of the laptop. If he dug any further, it could attract undue attention. The newly formed Federal Paranormal Task Force had been cracking down on smaller county departments lately, trying to stop illegal magic up and down Highway 95. His department, in particular, since the Taylors had such a reputation. Trey's prying could trigger their attention, and he didn't need that on top of whatever else his mate had gotten into. He didn't want to bring that type of scrutiny to their town.

His wolf perked up in warning, and Trey raised his head from his laptop in time to see Ness fly by him in her new car. He shook his head and chuckled, turning on his lights and going after her. She pulled over, and he exited the truck, adjusting his clothes. He took a deep breath and hid his smile, debating how much to aggravate her.

His wolf whined when he arrived at her door. He could feel her distress even without the animal. Her face was flushed, evidence of tears in her red eyes. He leaned down into her open window.

"What's wrong, baby girl?" he asked her softly.

She put her head down on the steering wheel. "I fucked up, Trey," she whispered.

"Get out the car."

He couldn't help the dominance in the order. Ness pulled it out of him effortlessly. She obeyed, and he pulled her into his arms the moment she stepped out. She shivered before wrapping her arms around him, a sob tearing from her. His wolf lost it, clawing at him to mark her and take her home to care for her. But he well knew his mate. That wouldn't work.

So, he held her, his heart ripping to shreds from her tears.

Trey rubbed her back and nuzzled into her neck, using his wolf's power to soothe her. It worked, and she stopped crying, shuddering in his arms.

"Tell me how to fix it, mama." He cupped her chin.

Her eyes were wet, her face devastated as she stared up at him. "I don't know if anyone can fix it. I'm scared to tell Nic what I did. They'll hate me."

"I really doubt that, baby girl. I ain't never met no riders like your cousins." He brushed her hair back from her face.

Her hair was loose, down around her shoulders, though disheveled from her crying. The edges were curling in the warm air, but she was no less beautiful. She looked away before settling her head on his chest.

"Want to come home with me so we can talk about it?"

She clutched him tighter and rubbed her face against his chest. "You're working."

His wolf rolled over for her. "Fair point. I was gonna pop up on you tonight anyways. You can tell me then, and we can figure out how to tell your cousins. Will that work?"

She bit her lip and studied his face. He used his thumb to free her lip from her teeth before leaning down and dropping a light kiss on her mouth. The leopard print top she wore was low cut, giving him an excellent view of her cleavage from this vantage point. He traced her collarbone with his fingers, humming in approval.

"You gone cook for me?"

She snorted. "I just made you brownies."

"And they were amazing, but that's not dinner." He nuzzled her cheek.

A tear slid down her face, and she squeezed him tight before stepping back.

"This," she waved a hand between the two of them, "will be so bad for you, Trey. I keep trying to save you from yourself."

He smiled and kissed her harder, backing them up until she was leaning against her car. His wolf bucked for more, but he held the animal back. It didn't stop him from sliding his hand into her tight jeans to cup her ass. Lord have mercy, this woman was too fucking fine to be real. He stepped away before he was tempted to say fuck work altogether.

"My wolf ain't trying to hear all that, ma. Now get in the car." He helped her into her car. He tapped the top as she buckled in. "Keep it under eighty, church girl."

She smirked and shook her head. "Thank you, Joseph."

"Anything for you, kitty cat. You'd know that if you stopped running from me."

She licked her lips, her eyes widening at his words. He returned to his truck and got in, watching as she pulled onto the road. He sighed and gave serious thought to going through her credit card and phone records to see if he could find the source of her distress. Instead, he called dispatch and told them he was done for the day. He would shower and head over to his mate to find out for himself what was wrong.

He wiped a hand down his face and froze. He sniffed his arm again, his wolf rattling his chest with a growl. He recognized that scent. It was the witch who'd tried to gain entry into town the other day. Cursing, he called his deputy to get the name from the ticket. He would have questions by the time he got to Ness's house.

Ness slipped the cast iron skillet into the oven, her mind everywhere but on the food she made for dinner. She'd made the glazed chicken recipe enough to be able to do it in her sleep. She hoped Trey liked it. And there she went, cooking for him again. The man was wearing her down. It was cute. She thought back to being in his arms hours ago. Her cat had loved every moment of it.

"Are you going to tell Joe?" Patsy asked. *"You need to stop running from that boy."*

Ness sighed and turned the burner with the rice off. She stirred it and ignored her grandmother for the moment. It wasn't the best course of action because Patsy didn't care either way.

"It's time, Vanessa," Patsy scolded.

"Oh my God, Grandmother. Couldn't you have been this chatty when we were looking for who killed you?"

Ness had been fully prepared to let the police deal with Patsy's murder, but Nicole and Audrey had been bound and determined to get justice themselves. It had taken them months, and her grandmother had been silent throughout the whole process, only showing up once they'd found the culprit.

Patsy sighed. *"I done told you."*

"Yes, Grandmother, I know."

Patsy hadn't wanted her son to suffer because his wife had been the one to murder her. If it were up to Ness and Nicole, the woman would've been under the jail, but Uncle Brandon had been hit hard. Even after a year, he was still a shadow of himself, so she could understand her grandmother's silence. Still...she was so chatty now.

"Fine. You're not ready to listen."

It wasn't that she disagreed with her grandmother, but she didn't want to drag Trey into the shit she was going through. He was Sheriff now. What could he do to help that wouldn't affect his job, or his life, for that matter? It wasn't fair of her. Why would Patsy want her to blow up his life like that?

"It's time to get down to business, and you need your mate."

"You think I don't want him?" she whispered.

"Trust him, baby."

Ness growled.

"What's wrong?"

Ness whirled around, her heart thundering. It was Eli, leaning against the wall of the kitchen.

"How long have you been there?"

"Long enough to see you talking to your spirits," he said.

"What spirits?" she hedged.

He rolled his eyes. "You know Israel been clocked your friends."

She licked her lips, unsure what to say to that.

He chuckled and stepped fully into the kitchen. "A wolf scent-marked the fuck out of this property since the last time I was here."

He changed the subject, but he'd gotten off one complicated topic and on to another.

"It's not JT, either," he continued despite her silence. The charming smile he wielded so well tilted his full lips. "I don't want to start no trouble, of course."

"Now, why don't I believe that?" she muttered, turning back to finish dinner.

Eli chuckled again and moved closer to her. She could feel his animal as he neared. Israel and Eli wore their power with an ease she envied.

"I guess he's trying to put me in my place." He trailed a finger down her arm. "Tell him his lil' baby safe."

Ness sucked in a surprised breath at his words. The lion shifter had never indicated that he'd been interested in her. Would she have taken him up on it? Maybe? It wasn't like she made the best decisions.

"You can tell him yourself." Trey's voice carried the length of the kitchen, and her cat sat forward.

Eli's smile was all teeth, his lion lighting his eyes. Ness hurriedly stepped between the two predators, rushing to Trey's side and putting her hand to his chest.

"I made dinner for you," she soothed.

Trey pulled her closer, but his eyes never left Eli. Ness stood on her toes so she could meet his gaze. Instantly, his expression shifted from irritation to heat. It took her breath away.

"Sit, I'll fix your plate." She rubbed her cheek along his.

Trey grabbed the back of her neck and kissed her, his tongue tangling with hers as he ravaged her mouth. Her legs were weak when he pulled back.

"You gotta stop feeding people who show up at your door, kitty cat. That's how you get strays." Trey said it to her, but he was taunting Eli.

"Are you gon' fix my plate too?" Eli asked.

"Keep pushing me," Trey warned, his wolf lighting his eyes.

His body was tense beneath her hands. It was the first time Ness had seen Trey anything other than the affable person he'd been since she'd known him. This...possessive Trey was, unfortunately for her, a huge turn-on.

"Eli, cut it out," Audrey snapped from the door. "Why did Lucky send you? I'm staying the night here."

Eli finally tore his gaze from Trey's to meet Ness's eyes. She looked away, already knowing the time for holding out on her cousin was over. If she didn't tell Audrey, Israel would, or he'd ordered Eli to do it. She sighed.

"Lucky told me to be your shadow until he arrived, so I'll crash here." He shot Trey a mocking smile as he left the kitchen. "Even if a dog stank it up with his scent," he tossed out.

Trey bucked against Ness, and she gripped him tight. Eli laughed as Audrey pushed him out.

"I swear to God he and Israel get off on aggravating people," Audrey said, sighing.

"Sickening tails," Ness muttered.

Audrey snorted. "It smells good in here, but I don't want to be a third wheel if this is a date." She was peeking into the oven. "Oh, snap, that looks amazing too. I'll just take my plate to my room."

Trey's eyes swung back to Ness. "This a date, baby girl?" he asked her softly.

She cleared her throat, unsure how to answer that.

"*So damn stubborn,*" Patsy grumbled. "*I'll leave you for tonight.*" Her grandmother disappeared.

Audrey shivered and looked over at her in question. While she was able to see and physically talk to their grandmother due to her magic, for Audrey and Nicole, their interactions with Patsy were limited to dreams. So, though Audrey could feel the presence of another, she didn't know it was their grandmother. Ness just shook her head, not wanting to explain. She took a deep breath and braced herself. It was about to be a long night.

Chapter Ten

Ness loved to cook, especially for her family, and cooking for Trey was fast becoming a part of that. True to her word, Audrey had taken her plate upstairs, giving Ness another reprieve. But that still left Trey to tell. To stall, she'd intentionally kept the conversation light during dinner. Despite the initial tension, they both relaxed as they ate and conversed. Something about Trey's presence soothed Ness like nothing she'd ever experienced. He'd helped her do the dishes afterward, and that little bit of domesticity had reassured her that confiding in him would be okay.

Right now, they were sitting on her back porch, watching the moon rise. She'd tried to sit beside him on the wicker sofa, but he'd pulled her into his lap. She was fighting to relax her body amidst the temptation, shuddering at the feel of him under her. Her cat was ready to jump his bones, and though she was moving reticently, she also wanted to.

"Tell me what's going on, Ness." His deep voice broke the silence as he slid his hand down her back in a gentle caress. "Talk to me, kitty cat."

She sighed and laid her head on his shoulder. She inhaled, taking in his scent, and settled more comfortably. When did she get so comfortable in his presence?

"I wonder if my life would be different if we'd met in high school," she murmured to stall.

He chuckled. "Mama was on us like a hawk in them days. School, practice, home. That's all she really allowed."

Ness hummed. He'd been a big deal in their high school, and though he'd been a couple of years ahead of her, she'd noticed him. Football was a huge thing in their county, and as the star player, Trey was well-known by everyone.

"You probably don't know this, but your father once warned me off you."

He growled and lifted her head. "Run that back to me." His brows were furrowed, his body tense beneath her. She didn't know why he was mad about something that had happened damn near fifteen years ago.

"What do y'all call him? The Colonel? I don't know why he singled me out at the time. I wasn't even with the girls that were talking about you."

She didn't want to tell him the exact words his father had given her, but it had stung. That was back when she'd still given a damn what people outside her family thought of her. She had no such illusions now. The only people that mattered to her all carried her last name.

"What did he say?"

She shrugged. "Just told me my family was trouble, and I wasn't good enough for you. It was silly because honestly, I was just trying to make it through high school in one piece."

It was her turn to frown as she took in his expression. He was angry. She smoothed out the lines on his forehead.

"It was eons ago, Trey. It's not worth being angry over."

"Is that why you've been running from me?"

Ness sighed. "His words may have hurt my feelings, but I believed them wholeheartedly at the time. Hell, the years have made them even more truthful. I got so much shit going on, Trey. I don't want to drag you into it."

"I'm your mate, Vanessa. Why the fuck would I leave you to deal with anything on your own?"

Oh, he was *mad* mad, calling her by her full first name. His words sent a shudder of need through her. Her grandmother had told her. Hell, her cat was now telling her, but...

Trey sucked his teeth. "God, you stubborn as hell. I'm not finna let you piss me off tonight. I already gotta deal with my daddy."

"You don't have to deal with the Colonel. I'm over it, Joseph." She wrapped her arms around his waist and cuddled into his chest.

"Well, I'm not," he snapped before taking a deep breath. "I'm sorry. I don't want to direct it at you."

She smiled. He was ready to ride for her about something that happened forever ago. It was...an amazing feeling. Something about it made her feel more secure than any promise any man had ever made to her. He wiped a hand across her hair.

"Back to you. Tell me why you so stressed. I'm at my limit for allowing it."

She hid her smile because he was very earnest. "Oh, you've been allowing it all this time?"

"Vanessa," he warned.

She traced his brows, amused by this man. She didn't think she'd ever seen him grumpy, never mind this anger he displayed. She liked it. Did that make her a bad person? Probably. All that power swirling around him was an aphrodisiac.

"Talk," he gently ordered.

She sighed. "I got into some trouble a few years ago."

"I've seen your rap sheet," he told her.

Embarrassment heated her cheeks.

"No judgment, remember?"

She nodded and cleared her throat. "Well, after the last time, I tried to go straight. I changed my name, moved north, and finessed a job at this insurance company authenticating and appraising art and antiques."

His eyebrows winged high, but he said nothing, so she continued.

"It paid well, so for the most part, I was able to stay out of trouble."

He snorted. "For the most part? You know what, never mind, keep going."

She tucked her smile. "Then a couple of spirits attached to this object asked to be returned to the rightful owners. That's how it started. After that, word got out, and I started taking side jobs from people to get their stuff back from thieves."

It was a little more complicated than that, but for brevity's sake... and to keep some of her secrets to herself, she didn't tell him everything. He'd promised not to judge, but she didn't want to risk it.

"They hired a thief to steal back their objects?"

She nodded. "It was easy, for the most part. But then..."

"Then?" he prodded.

Fuck it. She needed to get it all on the table. "So then, someone from a...big religious organization contacted me about an object — a holy relic. I don't know...the money dazzled me. I stole it, not knowing it belonged to this powerful warlock who worked for the paranormal task force."

She shivered. The number of spirits connected to that cross still gave her nightmares. If she had to do it all over again, she probably would — even knowing the trouble it had caused. It hadn't belonged to Zane and allowing him to keep it would've been more dangerous. What he'd been doing with the relic... She'd done a good thing, and no one could convince her otherwise.

Trey whistled. "I've had some experience with that task force."

"So, yeah, when I got the summons from Grandmother's estate, I left town, shed the identity I was using, and hoped to hide here."

"But they found you?"

She nodded. "And Zane wants to take this land as payment for what he lost."

"Your family ain't going for that," he stated softly, his face bunched in concentration.

"You don't have to tell me that."

He sighed. "Lord, baby girl. I'm gonna spend the rest of my life keeping you busy, so you'll stay out of trouble," he mumbled, but he didn't sound mad.

"You're not bothered by this?"

He snorted. "You've hung around the Taylors your whole life, Ness. Hell, you probably learned some of them thieving tricks from my family. What I look like judging you?"

She had learned many tricks from the Taylors, but she didn't think he actually wanted confirmation of that.

Trey shrugged. "I'm not squeaky clean, Ness. You did what you felt you had to do to get by. You a Fouche at the end of the day, and y'all all got this skewed sense of justice."

Surprisingly, amusement bubbled, and she laughed. "You act like you know me or something."

He smiled, and Lord, her whole body lit up.

"I know my wolf, and he got good taste in women."

"And the man?" she asked softly.

He chuckled. "The man gets distracted by a big ass and gorgeous face."

She laughed. "My ass ain't big."

"You a lie," he said, cupping said ass. "Don't worry, I can handle all this."

She sucked in a sharp breath as desire swamped her body. He inhaled deeply, and his eyes turned into those of his wolf.

"You distracting me, mama. Finish the story."

Her heart was racing, and she wasn't sure she could say anything, never mind finish a cohesive thought.

Trey gripped the back of her neck and nipped her chin. "Tell me so we can take care of all this heat."

He kissed her and Ness pressed against his mouth, not wanting him to end the kiss. She swiped her tongue out, and he opened his mouth to take her in. Trey's body was tense, tight with need for her. He pulled back, breathing hard.

"Finish," he whispered against her lips, his hand tangled in her hair. He'd already envisioned all the ways he would grip the long strands as he fucked her. He was at the end of his concentration, his wolf in total agreement.

She shuddered, cupping his cheeks. "There is nothing else. He's been watching my family, and I guess he'll go after them if we don't give up the land."

That was no small thing, and Trey understood her worry, but damn if he could think past the heat building between them. He forced his mind back onto the subject.

"Him or the Feds?"

She shrugged, squirming in his lap. She stood and straddled his legs, the short dress she wore lifting and exposing her thighs. God almighty, he would fuck her until neither of them could walk. The woman made his head spin. The puma that dwelled within her skin reached out to his wolf and communicated needs the woman was scared to voice. It tempered him slightly.

"Are you going to tease me and then leave?" Ness pouted, rubbing her heated sex against his erection.

He collared her throat with his hand. His claws had escaped his control, the tips of them pressing into his mate's delicate skin. She hissed and closed her eyes, the scent of her arousal rising between them.

Fuck, he was done.

This woman would own every part of him, and there was nothing he could or even wanted to do about it.

"You want me or just something to fuck on?" he asked, giving her her words back.

She shivered, and her power rose, sending goosebumps across his skin. "I want you, Joseph Taylor the Third."

It was his turn to shiver.

He stood, holding her to him tightly. Her legs wrapped around his waist, and for a moment, he considered taking her against the side of the house. That's how frenzied she had him. Instead, he entered, following her scent to her bedroom, kicking the door closed. He was aware that they weren't the only ones in the house, and it was another reason he hadn't taken her outside under the moon. Ness cupped his cheeks, bringing him down into a kiss. This was different than any they'd shared before. He could feel the depth of her feelings, the mask she'd been hidden behind wholly down.

His wolf reacted to her magic, filling him, the power reaching out to her puma. He wasn't leaving her bed until she was fully tied to him, soul to soul. Ness was his, and he was done letting her fight it.

Chapter Eleven

Trey set Ness down on the bed and pulled off his shirt. She watched him, licking her lips, her eyes dark with hunger. By the time he unsnapped his jeans, she was scrambling to get out of her clothes. There wasn't any talking, just a heavy tension that thickened the air between them.

Trey hissed when she pulled up the dress she was wearing. Her body was built by God especially for him. From every dip and curve to the long expanse of beautiful brown skin, Trey was obsessed with it all. He wound his finger in a circle, and his mate understood, turning her body. He moaned. How could he not? She was gorgeous.

And all his.

He pulled her to the end of the bed, eyeing her dewy center. He traced his claws down the skin of her thighs, highly satisfied with the welts that formed.

"Trey," she whispered, arching her back.

"Patience, baby girl. Let me look my fill," he murmured.

He kissed her from her ankles, nipping along her skin until he reached the apex of her thighs. He closed his eyes, inhaling her scent, his chest rumbling in hunger. Ness moaned loud and long the moment he kissed her sex. Her hands caressed his head, holding him in place as he devoured her. The taste of her was ambrosia, and Trey knew he would never get enough.

He used his hand on her stomach to hold her in place as he ate her pussy, his tongue swirling and dipping, thrashing across her clit as she moaned. She was squirming beneath him, her legs tightening around him and her stomach clenching under his palm.

"Shit, I'm coming, Trey," she whispered.

Trey went harder, sucking her clit into his mouth. Ness gripped his head and moaned as she came. He gentled his tongue until she relaxed, kissing his way up her beautiful body. He nuzzled into her soft stomach, leaving their combined scent along her skin. She pulled at his ears until he complied with her demand. He shared her taste with her, and she moaned into his mouth.

"You done running, mama?" he asked, gripping his dick, circling her entrance.

Ness lifted her hips, trying to slip him in before he was ready. He pulled back, and she whimpered, her full lips pushing out in an enticing pout.

"You said you wouldn't tease," she complained.

He nipped her shoulder, his wolf pushing for more. "I said no such thing."

Trey slid his dick across the folds of her sex, and Ness hissed. Unable to wait himself, he pushed forward, burrowing through her clenching pussy. Trey lifted his head, wanting to look her in her eyes as he connected them. She contracted tightly around him, and Trey bit down on his bottom lip to keep from moaning. He knew her shit would be fire, but the way her warm, wet walls surrounded his dick was beyond that. She threw her head back and moaned, exposing her elegant neck.

Ness rolled her hips, taking him deeper and welcoming him inside her. He started his strokes slow, savoring every slide. She pulled him into her, wrapping her thighs around his waist. Skin against skin, they reveled in each other. Their moans and sighs filled the air, no words needed between them. Magic swirled around them and trapped them in a cocoon of warmth.

His strokes were leisurely, their kisses decadent as they made love. Emotion tightened his chest, affection and possession tethering them together.

"I can't stop my wolf from binding us," he whispered desperately as the animal's power wrapped around them. "Tell me I can have you, baby girl."

He knew it was fast, and they had so much to learn about each other, but the thought of not tying this woman to him had panic speeding his strokes. Vanessa was capricious and ethereal, a spirit that couldn't and wouldn't be contained. He understood that about her and knew that holding her would be a balance of harnessing that wildness within her and allowing it freedom. If he let her overthink, she would run, if only to prove that she could.

The choice to bond had to be hers. No force on Earth could hold her if she didn't want to be held.

"Choose us," he whispered, lifting her leg so that he could hit deep.

Ness hummed in approval, gripping the sheets as he stroked against the spot that would send her over the edge. Trey nipped her skin harder than before, the bite of pain reaching her puma. The cat glowed in her eyes, answering his bid for submission.

"I'm yours, kitty cat, let me be that," he coaxed. He was unrelenting in his strokes, feeling her pussy contract tightly around him as she neared her climax.

"Trey," she hissed.

"Say yes, Ness." He sucked on her neck. "Stop running from us."

Her pussy clamped down, and Ness screamed as she came. Her arms wrapped around him tightly. He stroked her through it, not letting her come down.

"Yes," she panted, canting her hips as he deepened his strokes.

"Tell me," he demanded. With his wolf riding him, there was no more gentle. He fucked her with deep, hungry strokes, chanting her name.

"I'm yours," she moaned.

She tilted her head to the side to give him room, which was all the signal he needed. Trey dropped his head to her shoulder and lowered his canines. He was damn near drooling as he licked across her skin.

There was no fear as Trey clamped down on her shoulder with his teeth. The pain was expected, but her cat reveled in it. Ness's body was on fire as his power engulfed her. Her magic responded, happily tying their souls together. She scraped her nails down his back, needing to leave her own mark on Joseph Taylor. She didn't want any mistakes about who he belonged to. Ness had never been possessive a day in her life, but this? She would burn down the world behind this man.

Her stomach clenched, her clit throbbing as Trey fucked her harder. He licked across his bite, and her body shuddered in pleasure. It was like he knew her body better than she did. He controlled her ecstasy, his every stroke hitting just the right note. He plucked her clit expertly, and her body sang for him.

"Mine," he growled, looking up.

The wolf was in his gaze, light emitting from his dark orbs as he smiled, her blood still on his fangs. That...should not turn her on, but it sent her body straight into orgasm. Trey growled roughly, kissing her as his body stiffened as he came with her. They panted, his heavy weight on top of her. She loved the feeling, tightening her legs around his waist so he wouldn't move. She slid her hands up and down his back in gentle strokes, closing her eyes. Her body felt like putty. It was the most delicious, lethargic feeling.

"I can feel you inside me," he murmured against her shoulder.

She hummed, unable to articulate anything really. She still needed to tether her body to Earth before she was able to talk. Trey rolled them over, and she whined in objection.

"I'm too heavy, mama," he told her.

"I like your weight," she said, nuzzling against his chest.

They were both sweaty, and Ness loved the sensation against her skin. She kissed the spot over his heart, sighing in pleasure. As though waking from a dream, she realized that the writing in the middle of the tattoo on his chest was her name. The whole thing was encircled by protective runes.

"Trey," she whispered, tracing it.

He kissed the top of her head. "I told you, kitty cat. I was preparing myself for you."

Tears clogged her throat. She bussed a soft kiss on the tattoo. Feeling the power of it, she stiffened.

"Who you let put a spell on you?" she snapped.

He gripped her tight, keeping her from pulling away from him. "Calm your jealous ass down."

"Who, Joseph?" She probed the magic but calmed when she realized its signature. "Nicole?"

He nodded. "She said your grandmother ordered her to do it."

She took a breath to calm her racing heart. He was right to call her jealous, but doing magic, the type embedded in Trey's tattoo, was personal. She didn't like the thought of him trusting someone that much, especially someone *not her*. She settled her body comfortably on his chest.

"I didn't know," she muttered.

"You weren't supposed to." He rubbed his cheek against her hair. "How you feel?"

She knew what he was asking. She closed her eyes and examined the bond between them. It was intense, a vibrant rope tied between their souls. She could find no room for regret, only finding satisfaction and safety in her feelings.

"I guess being tied to you is okay," she joked instead.

He snorted. "I tied down Vanessa Fouche. Nobody can tell me shit, personally."

"You are ridiculous." She laughed. "But seriously, I don't want to overthink it. I just want to enjoy being in your arms, knowing you're my person."

"I like the sound of that," he murmured.

He turned his body, wrapping her in his arms as he stood from the bed.

"What part of enjoying being in your arms didn't you understand?" she complained as he headed to the bathroom with her hanging off of him.

"You're still in my arms."

She sighed and rolled her eyes. He put her down in the bathroom, and she walked over to the shower, starting it for them. The hot water felt good against her skin moments later when they got in. They took turns bathing each other, the intimate act tightening her chest with emotion. She looked forward to spending her life with Trey. It almost seemed silly running from him — until she remembered why. Her body stiffened.

"Aht-aht," he fussed, kissing her shoulder. "Leave that for tomorrow."

She relaxed as his hand cupped her pussy. He pressed his hardened dick into her back before turning her to face the wall.

"It ain't enough room in here for all that," she fussed, though she arched her body to give him the right angle.

He didn't utter a word, simply humming and fitting his dick right where they both wanted it. Ness closed her eyes and shuddered as he slid inside. Thoughts of tomorrow were replaced by need and lust as Trey made her forget everything but him.

"I hope you don't plan on sleeping," he whispered roughly in her ear.

Ness arched her back and closed her eyes tight as he hit her G-spot over and over. Her legs trembled, but it didn't stop her from winding her hips on his dick.

"That's it, right there, baby girl. Give me that shit."

The dominance in his voice settled over her, and her body followed his command. She laid her head against the cold tile, too overwhelmed to scream as her body melted. Her legs gave out, but Trey held her up, stroking once and then twice into her before he came, biting down onto her shoulder.

She hummed in satisfaction as he pulled out and turned her in his arms. He buried his head in the space between her neck and shoulder, licking over his mating mark.

"You're worth every second I had to wait," he murmured drunkenly.

She rubbed the back of his head, enjoying his affection. She wholeheartedly agreed with him. He was definitely worth the wait.

Chapter Twelve

The morning after a mating should've been reserved for pampering his mate, but Trey was up early, heading to his parents' house. Though his wolf was content, smug with their accomplishment, he couldn't get what the Colonel had done out of his mind. Knowing that the man had sabotaged his relationship with Ness way before she'd ever even crossed his radar was strange and pissed him off.

What could they have been by now without that interference?

It brought another point up to him. Had the Colonel and his mother known Ness was his mate, or suspected? If so, why hadn't they said anything to him? But...now that he thought about it, Patrice had never asked her son all the 'when will you mate' type of questions. She'd done it with his brother, but not Trey. He'd never put it together until now. Ness wanted him to let it go, but it didn't sit right with him to drop it without comment. He pulled into his parents' driveway, their large yard well-manicured, his mother's flower garden thriving from the many hours she spent there. Trey tucked his wolf's power and took a deep breath to clear his mind. He couldn't walk into the door accusatory.

His mother was knitting when he entered their home, in her favorite spot on the sofa, her gospel music playing softly in the background. He bent down and nuzzled the top of her head in greeting.

She smiled up at him before her eyes widened as she inhaled deeply. "Joseph. You did not."

He sighed, forgetting that his mate had properly marked him. Their scents had already merged. His wolf was taking nothing for granted and had bound them tight.

"Where's the Colonel?"

She put down her knitting. "Joe, that girl is bad news."

"That girl is my mate, and you've known that for years. I'll get to your part in keeping her from me," he warned her.

She looked away, a sure sign of her guilt. His stepfather came in from the back door, balancing a cooler in his hand. It was clear that he'd just come back from fishing. Though he was years removed from the army, Franklin was still fit. The bulk of muscle on his six-foot frame came from hauling lumber at the papermill in town and not lifting weights.

"Joe," the Colonel greeted.

"You told Vanessa she wasn't good enough for me." Trey didn't see any reason to beat around the bush. Franklin Harvey put down his cooler, in no rush to answer his stepson's accusation.

"She isn't," he said finally.

"That's not for you to judge. My wolf chose her...*I* chose her. She's mine, and if the two of you can't respect that, then there's no reason for me to be anywhere she's not welcome."

So much for coming in rationally. His anger spiked anew as his wolf mourned for all the time they'd missed.

"Joseph, you can't mean that." Patrice stood and rushed to him.

He stared at the man he'd seen as his father his whole life, waiting to see what he would say for himself.

"You don't know what that girl has probably gotten herself into."

"I got her regardless."

Franklin growled in aggravation. "She'll ruin your career."

"That's not your concern," Trey snapped.

"*You* are our concern," his mother added.

"So we're supposed to sit to the side while she blows through your life, stripping all the decency and hard work we've put into it?" Franklin argued.

"Stripping the..." Trey shook his head. "I'm not one for theatrics, so I'm not even going to entertain this conversation further. Keep your distance until you can treat my mate and her family with respect."

His mother gasped. "You would cut us off?"

"Let the boy go, Trice. He can learn the hard way," Franklin scoffed.

Trey stared at the inflexible man who had raised him and saw no give in his opinion. It would hurt, but he would never let anyone disrespect his mate. He left the house and headed straight for his Aunt Valerie's house. As he drove up, he noticed a bunch of people in the driveway. He sighed because he'd wanted to talk to his uncle alone. The Colonel was his dad, but Will had ensured his sister's eldest was raised to be a tough Taylor. His brother was able to mask around their parents, but Trey couldn't help but butt heads with Franklin.

He waved to some of his cousins as he got out and walked into the house. His aunt was at the sink mixing some fruit drink, probably for the number of kids that ran around outside.

"Auntie," he greeted, kissing her cheek.

She turned and hummed. "What's the matter, baby?"

"I wanted to talk to Unc."

His aunt Valerie stopped what she was doing and studied his face. "He in the back with the rest of them. What happened?"

He sighed. "Fighting with the Colonel."

Valerie let out a humph and turned the water off. "Nothing new, then." She cocked her head and took a deep inhale before a smile covered her face. "Oh, baby." She cupped his cheek. "Congratulations."

"Thank you, Auntie."

"No wonder my Ness ain't been around here. She out being fast," she joked.

He smiled, happy that someone other than him was excited about his mating.

"What you want to talk to your uncle about? Franklin not happy with your choice of mate?"

"Did you know he tried to run Ness off when we were in high school?"

She sucked her teeth and shook her head. "Chile, don't pay his ass no mind. He act like he ain't come from dirt roads and trailer parks his damn self. What did Ness say?"

"She say she over it."

Valerie held up her hand to stall him a moment. "Don't be slamming my damn door!" she fussed and then turned her attention back to him, putting a hand on her hip, picking up the conversation where she'd left off. "Then it's over, baby boy. But that don't mean you have to let him disrespect her in the here and now."

He nodded. "That's what I told them both."

"Then let it go."

He shook his head. "I told Mama I wouldn't talk to her until they learned to treat Ness with respect."

She gave him a soft smile. "Boy, I know Trice 'bout out her mind with worry."

"I can't go someplace where my mate is not welcomed, Aunt Val." Trey leaned against the counter next to the sink.

"And you have every right. But—" she held up her hand, "I will say this. Don't let it go on for too long. You know your mama wants what she thinks is best. If they haven't come around in a few weeks, I'll get Willie to go over there."

He gave her a droll look.

Valerie laughed. "You know your daddy hates my mate, so that'll straighten him up. I know you hate being at odds with your parents."

He nodded. It wasn't the first time his uncles had to see his dad about some shit.

"Congrats, baby, go get something to eat."

He nodded and walked outside. More cousins greeted him, and a baby was shoved into his arms. He bounced his cousin Amber's baby, smiling at her chocolate face. She was like a perfect doll. It made him think about the vision he'd shared with Ness. Now that they were bonded, it was closer, which pleased him immensely. He wanted that future with her.

"Nephew!" his Uncle Earl called out.

"What's up, Uncs?"

They all paused and inhaled.

"Well, I'll be damned," Willie said with a smile.

Earl laughed. "Done finally caught your Fouche, huh? Them jokers hard-headed, ain't it, Will?"

Willie laughed. "I guess he saw JT struggling with my mean ass daughter-in-law and wanted to join him."

"Aht-aht, don't be talking about my baby," JT said, stirring the coals in one of the grills.

"Congrats, Sheriff," Dante taunted from his seat.

Trey settled in an empty folding chair, propping the little one on his leg. He was happy he'd come by. It felt good to be in their company.

"How many cakes did you make?" Audrey fussed, balancing the cake dish she was carrying and closing the back door to Ness's car simultaneously.

Ness snorted but didn't answer. No matter how many she made, it was never enough for a Taylor kickback. The wolves liked to party and eat, and they never needed an occasion to get together and do so.

"You two been talking shit since y'all got in the car," she grumbled at her cousins.

"We ain't talking shit, you just don't want to hear us teasing you about your new mated status," Nicole laughed.

Same difference, as far as she was concerned.

"Trey done wore her ass out, now she taking her grumpiness out on us," Audrey teased.

"Not too much!" she snapped.

Which only made them laugh harder. She rolled her eyes and headed to the Taylor house. She could hear the music from the front yard, which meant the party was in full swing. Her cousins were partially correct. She was tired, yes, but more nervous than anything. In the time since Trey had left her house, her mind had gone through the gamut of emotions. She was happy to be mated to him. Her puma felt secure, and for the first time in her life, Ness felt optimistic.

Even with all the danger hanging over her head.

When Nic had called her about the Taylor kickback, Ness had been happy to have something to occupy her time. While she'd made cakes, she'd allowed her mind to wander over all the new possibilities her mating opened to her. The vision she'd seen in Trey's eyes had been the first thing to pop up. She wanted that image with everything in her.

So yeah, she'd been a little dreamy-eyed as she baked. It was a mistake letting her cousins see her that way. The two of them had had jokes from the moment they'd gotten in the car. The ride was barely ten minutes, and they'd managed to use that time to tap dance on every last one of her nerves.

"Look at that sway in her step, Nic. Her mate must be around here somewhere," Audrey teased behind her.

"I know Ms. Ma'am with the secret husband ain't still back there talking shit," Ness said over her shoulder.

Nicole cackled as they entered Ms. Valerie's house. Ness's smile widened when she saw her favorite Taylor standing over her sink. She loved every Taylor. They had saved her as a teenager. She'd spent a lot of her time over here getting into trouble with them. Hell, their Uncle Earl was the person who taught her to pick locks. But there was something about the no-nonsense she-wolf that had always soothed Ness. Valerie Taylor had never judged Ness or her mother, so Ness had never been afraid to talk to her.

At the time, she'd been mad at her family, thinking the curse was why her mother was on drugs. Ms. Valerie had been her comfort when she couldn't go to them.

"Is that my Ness?" Valerie asked with a wide smile.

Ness put down the cake she was carrying and grabbed the woman into a hug. She rested her head on her shoulder.

Valerie laughed. "Oh, now you wanna snuggle with me? You ain't had time for me when you was out here being fast."

"I always got time for you, Ms. Val," Ness told her.

She could feel the woman's wolf as it rubbed against her consciousness, offering comfort as she always did. It raised her puma, the cat responding to the maternal energy.

"Congratulations, baby girl. You marked him up good." Valerie stepped back and inspected the mark on Ness's shoulder. "Hey, girls."

Nic kissed Valerie's cheek. "Mama Val," she greeted.

"Your mate out there on the grill," Valerie told Nic.

Nic nodded, and she and Audrey headed out the back door toward all the noise and smells of food.

Valerie put her hand on her hip and studied Ness. "Finally stopped running from my nephew."

Ness laughed. "Wait now! Trey just started applying pressure. He was the one playing hard to get."

"A lie don't care who tell it," Valerie snickered.

"I was not the one running," Ness said.

"Mmmhmm. I'm glad y'all got it together."

Ness sighed. "He got a way about him."

"They all do, chile. Ain't no escaping a determined Taylor man. How you feel?"

"He's so good to me," Ness answered.

"And for you."

"That too," Ness had to admit.

"Dawn likes him. That's a plus," Valerie said.

"Mama's here?"

"Yeah, she look good too. Feels whole," Valerie commented.

Ness released a relieved breath. She'd long thought the same, but to have it confirmed by one of her mother's oldest friends felt good. If Valerie could feel it, it meant it was true, and hopefully not a fluke. She wanted to think the best of her mother and believe in her sobriety, but they'd walked a hard road, so there was still some residual doubt.

"Audrey's husband helped," she confided.

Valerie raised an eyebrow. "That's a fine man lil' mama snagged. I love that for her."

"Who fine? You ain't got no business looking at nobody," Willie said as he entered the kitchen and slapped his wife's ass.

"Excuse your damn nerve," Valerie said, though her eyes were twinkling.

Will walked around the table and grabbed Ness into a bear hug. She squealed and laughed as he picked her up like she weighed nothing. She loved this boisterous man.

"Congratulations, baby girl! You my niece for real now."

She smiled. "Thank you, Uncle Will."

He kissed her cheek. "Finally put my boy out of his misery."

Valerie cackled. "That's what I told her."

Ness rolled her eyes. "Y'all act like that man was pining for me."

"You better go save him from his cousins. They been teasing him since he came in here," Will told her.

Ness smiled and straightened, going to the back window of the kitchen. She spotted Trey laughing at something, a sleeping toddler cradled against his chest. Her heart knocked against her breastbone, and her breath stalled. He was so handsome, but with that baby in his arms, she could feel her ovaries fluttering. She wanted that with him so bad she could taste it. The image from their embrace came back to her in a wave. It had been her holding the baby, but the face was all Trey's. He would be such a fantastic father.

She swallowed the lump in her throat and turned from the window. Will and Valerie were clasped together, Will whispering in his mate's ear. She walked to the back door to give them privacy. The smells of food and the sounds of happy people washed over her, and for a moment, she felt guilt. She could possibly bring the feds down on all of this. It would change Springbrook forever.

Trey sensed her and looked up. He crooked his finger, and she immediately followed the unspoken order. He was in a lawn chair with his other cousins, in a semi-circle behind a couple of fryers that were going. Ness could already taste the catfish she knew was in there. Trey tugged on the hem of her shorts when she got to him, and she leaned over and kissed him. He traced the strings of her denim shorts.

"Where the rest of these shorts at?" he asked with a lecherous smile.

"In the store," she answered flippantly.

He licked his lips and tilted his head, taking in all of her. She wore a denim corset the same color as her cut-offs, and from the lust in his eyes, he liked it. His lascivious gaze heated her skin. She had to be careful around this many shifters this close to the full moon, but even with that pep talk, her stomach clenched in lust. Trey smiled wider, a hint of his fangs showing.

"Here go another one ain't got no clothes on," Dante called out from the other side of the circle.

It effectively brought her back down to Earth. "Shut yo ass up, Dante!" she barked out.

"Thank you because he get on my nerves," his sister said. "Gimme, Trey, I'll take her and lay her down."

As soon as his hands were free, Trey grabbed Ness and pulled her into his lap. "There, that's better." He nipped her skin. "I missed you."

She chuckled. "You just left my house a few hours ago."

"That don't mean shit," he murmured, rubbing their cheeks together.

Ness smiled, giddy on the inside.

"We'll talk about what you felt when you came out here later, okay?"

She sobered. "It's nothing."

He tipped her chin toward him. "No lying to me, kitty cat, especially now that we're mated. I don't like it."

"I don't want to talk about it. Is that better?"

"It's certainly honest, so I'll accept it for now."

She scoffed. Who did he think he was? He slid his hand inside her top, his skin warm against her back. He didn't do anything other than that, but it settled her cat.

"I have to tell my family," she told him.

He nodded. "Not tonight, though. We're running with the pack."

"We?"

He drank from his Solo cup. She grabbed it and sipped at it, wincing.

"The hell is in here?"

His cousins busted out laughing.

"Uncle Earl's moonshine," Trey answered, unsuccessfully hiding his smile.

"Lord have mercy," she coughed.

"I done taught you better than that, Vanessa Fouche," Earl called out.

"This one strong, Unc," she choked out.

They laughed at her again.

Trey pulled her mouth down to his and kissed her. "Tomorrow?"

She nodded. That gave her a momentary reprieve. She'd take as many as she could get.

Chapter Thirteen

The night was sticky, the humid air clinging to Trey's fur as his paws dug into the moist dirt of the forest. With his bond with Ness established, he saw the forest differently. Her magic boosted his senses, even allowing him to see the natural magic of their town. His wolf was happy, but that was not surprising. The animal was always delighted when Trey was in wolf form among his family. The pack run was his favorite thing, and now he got to share it with Ness. That brought a sense of satisfaction that had his wolf's head high as they traversed the dense woods.

He was toward the back, keeping an eye on his smaller, newly shifted cousins as well as the older wolves in the pack. He wasn't part of the pack hierarchy, but that didn't stop him from looking out for his family. It was in his nature to protect those he cared about. It was one of the reasons he'd flourished in his current job, even though his reasons for joining the police force hadn't been magnanimous at all.

His wolf darted ahead of the slower wolves to keep his wayward mate on the trail, snapping at her flank to keep the curious cat from veering too far. Her cat nipped back at him, playful and much more uninhibited than Ness in human form. He imagined this was what his mate would be like without the additional stress she'd endured for the past couple of years. He'd never intended to delay his pursuit of her for as long as he had and was kicking himself that she'd been dealing with her worries for so long without him.

They'd started the run at his Uncle Will's house, a natural progression from the barbecue. Even though some of them had been drunk, the metabolisms of their wolves had quickly burned off the alcohol. They'd been running and hunting for hours, avoiding the marshland around Springbrook. Now, though, Trey could feel the moon waning and his mate's exhaustion. He howled toward the front of the pack, letting JT know he was separating with his mate and her cousin. JT answered back, the sound carrying back to him in assent. He rubbed against Ness's flank, pushing her back toward her house, herding her and Audrey away from the pack. It didn't take them long to get to the Fouche property, his wolf passing effortlessly through the barrier they kept over the land.

He was surprised to see the warlock Audrey married waiting for them on the porch, his sharp gaze skimming his wife's cat. He hadn't been at the house when Trey had left this morning. In his wolf form, Trey could feel Israel's power in its raw essence, and he had to admit that he was impressed. Israel gathered Audrey, opened the door, and guided her in. Trey waited until the door was closed before he shifted, whistling for Ness's cat to come closer. The animal was still exploring the yard.

He sat down on the steps and waited her out. The puma loped to him, rubbing her fur against his legs. He butted heads with the cat, snickering as she licked across his skin, marking him with her scent.

"Come on, kitty cat, time to shift back," he ordered.

Her body shuddered a moment before he heard the cracking the Fouches went through to shift. He winced at the painful sound. It was a reminder that though she shifted, it wasn't like the natural shifters. Ness collapsed onto his lap, groaning.

Trey nuzzled into her neck. "You up for a shower?"

"Yes, please," she murmured, drunk with exhaustion.

He stood with her clutched tightly to his chest. She wrapped her arms around his neck, nuzzling and licking against his skin.

"Behave," he grunted.

She pouted, her hands stroking the back of his head. "Why?"

"Because you're exhausted, baby girl."

"Boo," she whispered.

He chuckled, closing her bedroom door with his foot. He walked them into her attached bathroom, sitting her on the sink. She leaned her head against the wall, her eyes closing, proving his point. He was gentle as he washed them off, forgoing clothes when he was done. He slid her into bed naked, pulling her into his chest as he got in. Ness lifted her leg and reached her hand down between them.

"Ness," he warned.

"Stop being stingy," she whispered, her hand wrapping tight around his dick.

It rose to her command, as it always would. The woman was everything in a mate he could've asked for.

"Please, Trey," she murmured, kissing along his neck.

"Oh, I got you begging for the dick, huh?"

Her sleepy sigh of pleasure as he slid in to the hilt melted him. He kept his strokes gentle, luxuriating in the feel of her surrounding him. Lazy sex with the woman he loved was a new level of intimacy, and he loved every minute. Their bodies moved in synch, their whispered words heightening the pleasure. Ness sucked on his neck, leaving marks all over his skin. Trey smiled and deepened his strokes, his thumb caressing her clit.

"Feels so good," she whispered, burrowing her head into his shoulder.

Trey pulled her closer, breathing in her scent as tingles started down his spine. "Now, baby girl," he ordered.

Ness arched her back, rotating her hips to take more of him. He pressed his thumb down harder, kissing her to swallow her moan as she crested. Her pussy tightened down on him, and Trey was done. He pushed in one final time as his climax swept him under. Her soft and even breathing brushed against his neck, and he could only chuckle. His spoiled woman. He gently separated their bodies and sauntered to the bathroom. He cleaned himself before wiping her down, tossing the washrag over his shoulder. He gathered his mate into his arms and settled, sleep easily overtaking him.

Ness was humming as she pulled out ingredients for Sunday dinner. It was her turn to host, and despite everything going on, she was excited about it. Trey was still asleep upstairs, and she had to admit that having him in her bed had quickly become her favorite part of the day. She'd worried that he'd bonded them too soon, but she wouldn't trade the feeling of him inside her mind for anything. Knowing that she could reach out and touch him soothed her tremendously, not to mention his occasional touches kept her puma calm inside of her.

She was down bad.

There was no other way to describe it. That man had her *gone* gone. He showed her he was the same, so she wasn't worried — not about that, at least.

"He's coming."

She yelped and dropped the peppers back into the vegetable drawer. She shut the refrigerator door and sucked in a surprised breath.

"What are you doing here?"

She already knew the answer. If she was seeing Monica in the middle of her locked house, it was because she'd died. Monica's magic was exceptional in life, and if anyone could find Ness from the other realm, it would be her. Even though they weren't friends, a pang of sadness hit Ness.

"How long do I have?"

She didn't bother beating around the bush. There was only one reason the witch would waste time visiting her. Monica shook her head, unable to answer that question. Ness understood there were rules around what a spirit could answer, but it was frustrating.

"I'm sorry. Did he...was it because of me?" Ness's shoulders slumped at the thought.

"Only partly. He knows he needs a lot of power to come after you and your family. I was convenient." Even in death, Monica was practical.

"Is he coming alone?" Ness asked, holding her breath.

"From what I could gather before he killed me, he was either on suspension or booted from the agency. I couldn't confirm either way."

"Babe," Trey called, entering the kitchen.

Ness turned to him and held up her hand, returning her attention to Monica. "Do you need me to help you cross?"

Monica smiled sadly but shook her head. *"I wanted to warn you and give you a better chance than I had."*

"Thank you," Ness told her quietly.

Monica disappeared as silently as she'd appeared, and Ness let out a heavy breath, leaning against the kitchen counter.

"What was that?" Trey asked.

"A warning."

"About the warlock?"

She nodded. "He's coming after me next."

He cursed. "We need to tell the family."

She swallowed and grabbed her phone. "Sunday dinner is here tonight. I'll call and tell everyone to make sure they're here."

He pulled her into his arms, lifting her chin. "I got you, hear?"

She nodded, though her throat was tight. "I'm so..."

He kissed her, cutting off her words. "Your cousins would never abandon you."

She knew that. She and her cousins had been through a lot in the last two years, but this... Ness took a shaky breath.

"You're right." She had to have faith in that.

He nodded and released her. Audrey and Israel were already here. They'd stayed the night after the pack run, so she went to work on calling the others.

"From what I could gather before he killed me, he was either on suspension or booted from the agency. I couldn't confirm either way."

"Babe," Trey called, entering the kitchen.

Ness turned to him and held up her hand, returning her attention to Monica. "Do you need me to help you cross?"

Monica smiled sadly but shook her head. *"I wanted to warn you and give you a better chance than I had."*

"Thank you," Ness told her quietly.

Monica disappeared as silently as she'd appeared, and Ness let out a heavy breath, leaning against the kitchen counter.

"What was that?" Trey asked.

"A warning."

"About the warlock?"

She nodded. "He's coming after me next."

He cursed. "We need to tell the family."

She swallowed and grabbed her phone. "Sunday dinner is here. I'll call and tell everyone to make sure they're here."

He pulled her into his arms, lifting her chin. "I got you, hear?"

She nodded, though her throat was tight. "I'm so..."

He kissed her, cutting off her words. "Your cousins would never abandon you."

She knew that. She and her cousins had been through a lot in the last year and a half, but this... Ness took a shaky breath.

"You're right." She had to have faith in that.

He nodded and released her. Audrey and Israel were already here. They'd stayed the night after the pack run, so she went to work on calling the others.

Chapter Fourteen

Ness didn't know whether she would throw up or run.

Both of those options were a possibility at the moment. She'd cooked all morning, using that to get her mind together. Should she wait until before or after dinner? What if, despite Trey's reassurance, her cousins stormed out? It wasn't like they wouldn't have the right to be angry. Hell, she'd be furious if either one of them had kept something so serious a secret from her. She'd literally torn into Audrey months ago for hiding a husband.

She was hiding a real and credible threat to the family.

That was way worse than a secret husband.

Fuck.

She sighed and continued cutting up vegetables for salad. What else could she do at this point? Her cousins were due in minutes, and Ness couldn't keep her hands from shaking. She looked up as Audrey came into the kitchen.

"What's wrong?" Audrey asked, posting up across from Ness. Her cousin studied her face, her magic probing.

"That's not fair," she muttered.

Audrey shrugged, unrepentant. "You've been keeping secrets, and I'm tired of waiting for you to come to me."

"I'll tell you along with everyone else. I don't want to have to tell the story more than once."

Audrey sucked her teeth. "Lucky already told me about your visit to Savannah to meet a witch."

Ness's stomach flipped, and she turned from her cousin's perceptive gaze.

"It's worse than that?" Audrey leaned forward.

Ness still didn't say anything.

"Vanessa Rene."

"Audrey Celeste."

Audrey sighed. "That corny ass name. I don't know what Kit was thinking."

Ness smiled for the first time since Monica had visited her. "Leave my auntie alone."

"So, since you won't tell me your secret, tell me about Sheriff Taylor."

"Why you gotta say it like that?"

Audrey snorted. "I just didn't see you with a cop. Does he know you steal things for fun?"

Ness cracked up laughing. "Whatever, bitch."

"Well?"

Ness shrugged. "He's amazing, and I'm kind of glad he took the decision to bond out of my hands. You know how I am."

"You don't overthink as much as Nicole, but it's close. How's the sex?"

"None of your business, married woman," Ness snickered.

"Please, y'all made it my business last night...and this morning," Audrey joked.

Ness's cheeks burned. "Leave me alone!"

Her cousin laughed, only tapering off because Trey entered the kitchen.

"Nah, finish y'all little conversation," he taunted, sitting at the kitchen table.

He lounged in the chair, stretching his lanky, muscular body out in a way that made her skin heat. Trey sensed it and gave her a smirk that clenched her stomach. God almighty, she was down bad.

Audrey shot Ness a mischievous look before turning to Trey. "Ness was telling me that you had a big—"

"Too much, Celeste!" She rushed to cut Audrey off.

Trey and Audrey both laughed. The front door opened, and she was saved by that. She hadn't heard a car, which meant it was her aunts. They always walked through the path between their houses when they visited. Shelby, Dawn, and Kit came in chatting, pausing as they entered the kitchen. Her aunts shared a look between them and snickered.

"Well, then," Shelby said, smiling at Dawn.

"Hey, baby," Dawn greeted.

Ness opened her mouth to return the greeting but realized her mother was talking to Trey and not her. She rolled her eyes.

"Hey, mama." Trey gave Ness a smug smile. She sucked her teeth at the both of them.

"Mama already, huh? I know that's right, nephew," Kit said, sitting beside him.

Ness already knew the women were finna drag it. She pinched her lips together to keep from saying anything that would add fuel to their teasing.

"You're the one that marked up Ness's yard, huh?" Shelby asked him, sitting across from her sister.

Trey smiled. "She had too many strays hanging around."

Dawn and Kit cackled.

"Speaking of one," Shelby said with a smile as the roar of motorcycles entered the yard.

The Taylors had arrived, and with their appearance, butterflies took off in her stomach.

"Leave my Dante alone," Dawn defended.

Dante came swaggering into the house no sooner than she'd finished the sentence.

"Is there gonna be food at this meeting?"

"Your greedy ass," Dawn said, standing. "I just got through defending you and look at the first thing you ask."

Dante grabbed her and lifted her into a hug. "Don't do me like that, mama."

"Trey called you a stray," Dawn instigated.

Dante chuckled. "Oh, he done finally caught his mate. Now he got jokes."

In the next ten minutes, the rest of her family filed in, and Ness decided it would be easier to tell them all before dinner. Taking a deep breath, she guided everyone into the living room and prepared to spill her guts. Trey came up behind her and wrapped his arm around her waist in support. He stood next to her as she faced her family.

Ness took a shaky breath. How to start?

"So... I need to tell you guys something." She looked to Trey. He nodded for her to continue. "The years before Grandmother died, I worked for this insurance company. I did appraisals and authentications."

"How did you get a job like that?" Dawn frowned. "No offense, but don't that require a college degree?"

All eyes were focused on her. Her cheeks heated.

"I forged the credentials." She shrugged.

JT and Dante snickered.

"Chile," Shelby muttered.

"Anyways, I was good at it," she argued but shook her head. She was avoiding the hard part. "If I came across stuff that was stolen, I started returning them to the rightful owners. Their spirits were attached, and it was starting to get to me."

It was Nic who snickered this time. "Return them how?"

"Okay, I stole them and returned them," she admitted.

"That sounds more like you than whatever 'appraising' means," her mother muttered.

"Mom."

Dawn held up her hands but kept quiet.

"I came across a religious artifact and suffice it to say that the church paid me a good…good amount of money to return it to them. I didn't know that the warlock that had possession of the artifact was a part of the Paranormal Task Force," she rushed out.

"You stole from the Feds?" Cellus asked, his eyes wide.

"Even for you, Vanessa, that's wild," her aunt Kit said.

Israel laughed but held up his hands when his wife elbowed him. "I'm sorry. It's not funny."

"Lord hammercy, are you beating around the bush to tell us that the Feds are after you?" Audrey shrieked.

"Us," she whispered.

"Now wait, how we get in it?" Nic asked.

Ness shared a look with Trey, scared to utter the last part.

"Spit it out so we can handle it, baby girl," JT told her.

Her shoulders dropped. "I can't steal back the artifact, so he wants something of equal power."

"Oh, do we get to steal from another museum?" Kit asked excitedly, sitting forward in her seat.

"Auntie, sit yo tail back. Y'all fast asses ain't helping steal nothing else," Cellus said with a laugh.

"Bev, you might want to leave the room for this part," Dawn warned. "What are we stealing?"

Ness's eyes watered, and she looked down, unable to face her family. Trey's hand was warm on her back, his breath blowing across her cheek as he whispered reassurances in her ear. She took a shuddering breath and lifted her head.

"He wants this land," she finally got out.

"The hell he does."

"I wish the fuck he would."

"Chile, please."

All three sisters spoke at the same time.

Ness caught her cousin's eyes, and Nicole didn't lower her gaze. "All of it, Ness," Nic ordered.

"I would never even so much as bargain with this land. But he has people watching the family."

"This family?" Audrey asked.

Ness nodded. "He had pictures. Even Julian," she admitted.

Cellus cursed and whipped out his phone, and the rest of the room exploded in sounds of disbelief.

"That was careless, Ness. We're talking about the Feds," Audrey said.

"You don't think I know that?" Ness argued. "I messed up! Happy?"

"Don't even think about storming your spoiled ass out of this room," Nicole warned her.

Ness's throat tightened with unshed tears, and she lowered her head again.

"Don't do that, Ness. We're not upset with you," Audrey tried to reassure her.

"So what do we do? Is he sending an army here to try and get the land?" Shelby asked, holding her hand up for silence.

"He sent someone here to bargain, but I told her no. She warned me that he was on his way, presumably to take the land himself. But she doesn't know whether or not he is still on the task force."

Israel nodded. "The magic imbued on this land is powerful. I may have tried to access it myself if I weren't married to Audrey."

"Now see, nephew. How are we supposed to keep defending you when you're so nonchalant about your foolishness?" Dawn asked.

Israel shrugged, unconcerned either way. "I'm just saying. A powerful warlock with the government's backing wanting this land is not surprising. Who is he?"

"Zane McIntyre," she answered.

Israel whistled, and JT cursed. She was sure he knew all manner of powerful warlocks.

"He worse than Iz?" Nicole asked her mate.

JT shrugged. "Worse? That's a toss-up."

Everyone turned their attention to the only warlock in the family.

"Hey, I'm a reformed man, thank you very much," Israel defended.

Audrey kissed her husband. "You're better for it."

"Better is debatable," JT muttered.

"Okay, let's focus," Bev said. "If he's not bringing charges, he can't order an army here, so we have that going for us."

Ness had used Cellus's wife, Bev, to get her out of many scrapes over the years, so she trusted the woman's words.

"Then we ain't got shit to worry about," Dante chimed in. "Can't nobody come to Springbrook without having to go through us."

Ness's pulse thundered as her stomach turned. "I'm sorry I brought this danger onto us."

"There's nothing to be done about it now," Shelby said.

"If that's the case, then I'm ready to eat," Dawn said, standing.

The rest of the family filed out behind her, leaving Ness dumbfounded. She'd expected a lot more yelling and screaming. Hell, even questions. Audrey and Nic each ran a hand across her shoulder as they passed her to eat.

"Quit stressing, baby girl. You know how we handle shit," Dante told her, dropping a kiss to the top of her head.

Trey sat in a vacated armchair and pulled her into his lap. He wrapped his arms around her and nuzzled her neck.

"Feel better now that it's out in the open?"

She took a deep breath. "Yeah, actually. I thought..." She shook her head.

She thought they would be way madder than they were. She knew she would've been pissed, but they accepted it...accepted her.

"Mistakes happen, love. But we fix them and move on. We'll tackle this together, and then when it's fixed, we get married."

She choked. "What?"

"I want a wedding."

"Why?"

"Something about claiming you in front of God and everyone appeals to me."

She snorted. "You left enough marks for the whole county to see I'm yours."

He rubbed one of those marks, a rumble of satisfaction rattling his chest. "Yeah, but I want all the trappings."

"All of them?" she asked softly, turning to straddle him.

"All of 'em, kitty cat. We can even put a picket fence up around this house."

Her heart melted. "We can make this our home?"

"My wolf likes it here, and I can feel your contentment. It feels different than the others."

She nodded. "I feel like my grandmother redid it with me in mind."

He hummed and licked her neck. "So, the house, three to five kids, the picket fence, all that. I want it with you, kitty cat."

She pulled his face up and kissed him, putting all her feelings into it. She loved him until her soul ached with it. She could almost understand why her aunt had tried resurrecting her mate from the dead. This type of love wasn't one that could easily be given up.

"I love you, Joseph," she whispered against his lips.

"I love you so very much, Vanessa," he told her.

"Come in here and eat, you two," her mother called from the kitchen.

She rested her forehead against Trey's, overwhelmed with relief. Yeah, they had to find a way to outsmart a powerful warlock, but she'd take on anything as long as her family was behind her.

Chapter Fifteen

Half of the week was gone already, and it had passed in the blink of an eye. He'd been moving his stuff into Ness's house all week at a slow pace, giving her time to get used to the idea. So far, he hadn't had any pushback from her, which was a good thing. He loved waking up to Vanessa beside him, and his wolf was comfortable. He couldn't ask for anything more. He knew that he'd rushed their mating a bit, but he couldn't have her thinking she was in the world alone. With everything on her plate, he wanted to be there for her.

The phone on his desk rang, and he frowned, not really in the mood for anything other than the paperwork littering his desk.

"Sheriff Taylor."

"Good afternoon, Sheriff, this is Lieutenant Sumner with the FPTF. Do you have a few minutes to chat?"

Trey frowned, wondering why someone from the Federal Paranormal Task Force would be calling to "chat." They'd been on his department's ass for the past few months for them to tighten up the illegal magic trade that flowed through their territory via the I-95 corridor, and now he wanted to chat? His mind flashed to the warlock after Ness, and he got anxious. Could McIntyre still be working with the feds?

"What can I do for you?"

"There's been rumors about a warlock, Zane McIntyre. Have you had any dealings with him lately?"

Trey leaned back in his chair, intrigued. "Can't say that I have."

Ness had told the family yesterday that the spirit who'd visited her thought McIntyre had been booted from the task force. Why, then, was Sumner calling him about the warlock?

"So, he hasn't contacted your department at all?"

"What's this about?"

There was a moment of tense silence before Sumner sighed. "If you get any communication from that person, he is no longer affiliated with our department."

"Are you warning me about something in particular or just giving me a personnel change?"

"We got word of some activity that was outside of how we operate. Rumors have him possibly heading your way. I thought I'd do you the professional courtesy of giving you a heads up."

Trey had a feeling he was holding a lot more back than he was saying, but Ness had given him a pretty good idea of the warlock's power.

"So, if I run into this warlock, is he likely to be alone?"

That was the most pressing question the family had, and it was a valid one. Knowing that McIntyre wasn't headed their way with the power of an army behind him was already a relief.

"I can't really say. This job puts us in contact with any number of paranormals. Who's to say if he's gathered a gang of his own?" Sumner reluctantly answered.

"Understood," Trey told him.

They ended the call, and Trey sat back, contemplating what to do with the information. The warning was a surprise and one he would heed. The static from the radio on his desk sounded, drawing his attention.

"Sheriff, we got a rogue bear in the middle of the mall parking lot," his deputy called.

Trey cursed and rushed from his office. He prayed that they could contain the shifter there. The outdoor mall parking lot was generally empty this early in the morning, but it wouldn't stay that way for long. Once the stores started opening, people would begin filing in. He sped through town, cursing anew when he saw the number of deputies surrounding the bear shifter. He recognized the bear. Bryant Jackson had lost his mate a few years ago, and Trey understood that losing a mate could sometimes cause a sort of insanity. But from what he'd observed, the farmer had been dealing with it fine until now.

Trey's wolf wanted to come out and deal with the bear, but as sheriff, he needed to think with his head instead. The power he'd gained when mating with Ness filled him enough that as he looked at Bryant, he could tell that something other than normal mate sickness was affecting the bear. There was a tinge of magic surrounding the shifter, and Trey knew his first call would be to their resident magic experts when he got the situation under control.

Trey jumped from his truck and hand-signaled to his deputies to surround the animal. He then rushed to the back, where he kept all his magical supplies. Pulling out the tranquilizer gun, he rummaged until he found the tranqs the department kept on hand for such emergencies. He rounded the truck and sucked his teeth as one of his deputies lost control of their animal, shifting and jumping at the farmer.

The two beasts clashed and tumbled across the parking lot, busting through the ring of deputies surrounding them. His job was made significantly more complicated because he couldn't tell the two black bears apart. His claws slipped out in his frustration, and he struggled to hold the gun still. He could possibly take the shot, but it would possibly hit his deputy and not Bryant.

They slammed into two different cars before Trey made his decision. He used the hood of his car to line up his shot and took aim. He shot once, hitting one of the bears in the flank before loading and shooting the other. Both bears seemed to freeze in place before slamming hard onto another car. Trey winced. He knew the owners of the damaged vehicles would be cursing when he sent deputies to inform them of the damage.

"Load them up!" he ordered his deputies, sighing because moving two three-ton bears was not on his agenda for the day.

Trey grabbed blankets from the back as both men thankfully shifted back into their naked human forms. As he walked over to the downed shifters, his gaze caught sight of a lone man standing a distance away from the melee. The male leaned against a car, his eyes firmly glued to the situation. Who was he? Whoever it was raised his wolf's hackles, and Trey paused what he was doing. He didn't have time to get distracted. There was only so long the tranqs would last, so he shook off the curiosity and went back to handling business.

It took them about half an hour to get both men back to the station. He was sweating and praying he had remembered to dry clean the extra uniform he kept in his office.

"Get Bryant's daughter on the phone," he ordered the dispatcher at the front desk.

An hour later, done consoling the bear's grieving daughter, he promised to get her father help and allow him to sleep the madness off in the cell. The farmer had woken and was back in his bear form, currently slamming into the bespelled bars that kept him confined. Trey let out a relieved sigh when Shelby and Nicole rushed into the jail attached to the department.

"Sorry it took so long," Shelby told him, lugging a canvas bag he knew contained the tools she needed to do magic.

There had been many things he'd learned about the town when he took the job. The briefing he'd gotten from the former sheriff was full of secrets and tricks and tips about doing the job in a town like Springbrook. Namely, he hadn't known how much the Fouches did to keep the county in check. He'd understood that they kept some of the more unsavory elements from the town, but he hadn't been aware that they actively worked with the sheriff's department.

The tranqs were one example of how they helped keep the officers in the town safe from magic. The fact that dispatch had called Shelby before he got a chance to told him how integral the family was to their work. There were protocols in place that the Fouches had established. It was the reason the Fouches had such sway and power in the area. They weren't selfish with it and used it to help anyone in Springbrook and Westport, the neighboring town.

"You're fine. The tranq worked for a while. There was something I wanted to talk to you about, anyway," he told her, smiling when he spotted Nicole behind her aunt.

"Hey, Trey!" She had her own canvas bag.

"Are you taking Ms. Shelby's place?"

"Learning the ropes," she replied, her eyes widening as Bryant slammed into the bars.

Shelby hummed and narrowed her eyes. "I thought he was past the madness."

"I think something triggered it." Trey crossed his arms over his chest. "I saw something in his...aura, maybe? I haven't quite grasped the magic I got from my mating with Ness yet."

Shelby hummed again as she studied Bryant. "Any of your deputies hurt?"

"A couple of scratches. I had medical look over them," he answered.

He hovered over the small women as they got to work. It was fascinating to see them use their powers, especially now that he could see the magic they were wielding. It was a light show to him, and it raised his respect for their powers.

The women were exhausted when they were done, but it had worked. Bryant was in his human form, sitting dazed on the end of the bench in the cell. Shelby walked up to him.

"There was a spell over him, but I don't know the source," Shelby told him in a tired voice.

"I'll get a deputy out to his farm to look around. He's one to mind his business, so I can't imagine how he got into something." Trey made a mental note to send Deputy Thomas out that way. "What do you think?"

"He'll be fine in a day or so. Did you call his daughter?"

"I already talked to her. She's okay letting him stay here until it passes." He shrugged because that was all he could do.

Shelby gripped his shoulder and walked away to repack their supplies as Nicole approached him.

She wore a tired smile. "How are you and Ness doing?"

He smiled, always happy to talk about his mate. "We're getting there."

"Are you worried about this warlock?" She studied his face.

"Worry don't help none," he said with a shrug. "I've been on the phone with Israel about it."

Audrey's husband had wanted a breakdown of Trey's jurisdiction so that he could put up a locator spell for McIntyre. The spells were illegal, so Israel needed to make sure that he was careful to keep it contained to the three cities that made up Westport County.

"He and Audrey will probably come down and stay here until it's done. You'll have to share your honeymoon time with them." She waggled her eyebrows.

He laughed at the silly woman. "We'll be alright."

"I learned something from Titi Shelby..." she trailed off, her eyes studying him.

He assumed she was waiting for some type of reaction from him, but he waited her out.

She sucked her teeth. "You are no fun! Ness said it was hard to rile you, but I thought she was exaggerating."

"I knew y'all were shit starters on purpose," he teased.

She laughed. "Anyways! Aunt Shelby told me my grandmother knew you and Ness were mates from when y'all were kids."

This time, Trey frowned. He'd suspected his mother knew something, but not that. "I...wait, explain it to me."

"Titi!" Nic called out, gesturing for her aunt. "You said that Grandmother told Ms. Patrice about Trey and Ness being mates?"

Shelby sucked her teeth and nodded. "I swear, that woman."

"Why didn't Ms. Patsy say anything to me?" Trey asked, getting mad at the secrecy. He'd met their grandmother on more than one occasion. Why hadn't she mentioned anything to him?

"It depends." Shelby shrugged. "If your mother told her not to, Mama would've honored that. She wasn't one to push her power on anyone. And you know how your mother is."

Trey sighed because he absolutely knew how his mother could be. He was stunned that she would go this far to interfere in his life. It was already bad enough that the Colonel had stepped to Ness when she was young, but this was too far! He nodded as the women left, shock keeping him from following them out. What did he do with this new information? He wanted to confront his parents again, but he'd already seen how little it would affect them. Did he tell his mate this information? That was the more pressing question.

Chapter Sixteen

Ness swayed to the music she had playing in the kitchen, her mind for once not on the upcoming danger to her family. Instead, she was daydreaming. Being mated to Trey was better than anything she'd ever dreamed of. For many years, when she'd been going through the turmoil with her mother, her safe haven had been her daydreams. She'd wanted a family and a stable home, and she would spend a lot of hours imagining what that would look like. Trey exceeded all those visions.

The front door opened, and her heart fluttered. He was home, and though she'd been busy at the brewery today, she'd missed him.

"In here, babe," she called out to him.

He came around the corner in different clothes than what he'd gone to work in. The simple jeans and sheriff's department t-shirt looked well-worn and hugged his muscular body in a way that heated her from the inside out. He swaggered over to her as she turned off the stove. He hummed in approval, his eyes skimming her body as he pulled her closer. She wore his t-shirt and nothing else.

"How was your day?" The words came out breathless.

He smiled down at her, dropping a soft peck on her lips. "Hectic, but none of that matters right now." He nuzzled into her neck, and her knees went weak.

"Go shower. I'll have the table set by the time you come down."

He hummed, his teeth raking down her skin. He gripped her chin and brought their mouths together. There was nothing gentle about the kiss he gave her. Trey devoured her, his tongue twisting with hers, his hunger blatantly traveling across their bond. She shuddered in need.

"You should join me," he murmured against her lips.

"You'll never eat if I do," she told him, running her hands up his back.

His erection pressed into her stomach, and the power of his animal surrounded her until it felt like a warm blanket of fur over her skin. She chuckled as he lifted her by her ass. Wrapping her legs around his waist, she cupped the back of his head and kissed him. Trey walked them up the stairs, not releasing her lips. He set her down on her feet when they reached her room. She headed to the attached bathroom and started the water for him. Crossing his arms over his chest and leaning against the door jamb, Trey watched her, his eyes heavy with lust.

"You gon' spoil me, baby girl," he murmured, pulling her between his legs.

She kissed him softly. "You got a problem with that?"

"Not at all." He scraped his teeth down her neck. "Being spoiled by the woman I love is no hardship."

Heat bloomed through her as her heart thudded. "Trey," she whispered.

"I've been in love with you long before I started pursuing you." He stared deep into her eyes, seeing past all the bravado she showed the world.

A tear slid down her cheek. "You mean your wolf?" She was emotional, yes, but him saying that made her want to swallow him whole.

Trey shook his head. "Even leaving him out of it," he swore.

He tried to lift her again, but she stepped back, going to her knees.

"Spoiling the fuck out of your man, huh?" The smile he gave her made her feel like prey.

She tilted her head, showing her neck, and he growled. A shudder wracked her body, moisture sliding down her leg. He closed the distance between them and gripped the back of her head.

"Show me how you feel, kitty cat," he said hoarsely.

Ness grabbed his legs, digging her nails into his skin until he hissed. In contrast, the kiss she gave his thigh was gentle. His dick bobbed in reaction, and she licked her lips in anticipation. She wrapped her hand around his shaft, humming at the soft firmness of it.

She greedily took him into her mouth, sucking roughly. Perhaps she could've gone slower, eased them into it, but he moaned, and Ness made it her mission to make him lose control. Trey cursed and crushed strands of her hair in his hand. The bite of it made her go harder. She took him deep until he touched the back of her throat. Tightening her grip on his length, she focused on the head of his dick, teasing him. His legs were shaking, and she went even harder.

"Up. Fuck... Up, Ness." Trey tried to pull back, but she sucked him into her mouth harder. "God damnit, woman," he moaned.

Ness didn't stop until he shouted as he orgasmed, coating her tongue. Trey pulled her up, ripped her panties from her body, and slid his still-hard dick into her.

"Water will get cold," she teased, pulling her shirt up over her head.

His next stroke was harder, and she gasped as goosebumps peppered her skin. "I'll never get tired of feeling this pussy wrapped around me," he murmured, slowly withdrawing. His head lowered as he watched.

Ness cupped his cheeks and brought him closer to her, fusing their mouths together. She knew Trey was fastidious, and it was no different when they made love. Her every gasp, the smallest tightening of her muscles, he noticed and kept cataloged. She held him tight as he fucked her meticulously, burrowing into her with powerful, sure strokes.

"Come for me, baby girl," he ordered.

Her body was his to control, and Ness could only scream as her climax shattered her body. She held him tight as he rocked into her, his groin rubbing over her clit every time he moved. She could already feel another orgasm building. Her heart raced, and her magic filled the room in reaction. The hair on the back of her neck stood up, and the edges of her vision went black as it finally crashed over her.

Trey bit into his mating mark and stiffened as he came. She could hear them panting over the running shower.

"You're trying to kill me, aren't you?" he whispered.

She closed her eyes, smiling. "That's you."

"I love you." He kissed her neck softly.

"I love you so much," she answered, sighing in pleasure.

Why did she wait so long to let this man catch her? Her insecurities seemed silly in the face of the bliss she felt in his arms. She promised herself that she wouldn't waste any more of their time together.

Trey was in a good mood, and his mate was a hundred percent the reason. Waking up beside her was now his favorite thing. It was why he was hunched over a motorcycle at his uncle's shop, listening to loud seventies soul and the shit-talking the other mechanics were doing. After his day yesterday, he didn't think he'd be in the mood to work in the shop, but when his uncle Nathan called, in a lust filled daze, he happily agreed—even though it meant leaving his warm bed.

He'd spent a lot of time in his Uncle Nathan's shop growing up. It was in Westport instead of Springbrook, and thus outside of his mother's watchful eye. His uncle had taught him everything he knew about motorcycles. Being a full-time mechanic wasn't the job for him, but because he worked for law enforcement, he used his skills to help his cousins conceal their more illegal contraband. He knew all the places they checked and helped them refit the bikes with better hiding spaces.

"Big brother!"

Trey looked up from the motorcycle he was working on, grinning as his little brother Richie sauntered into the hot shop. The two brothers were the same height, but Richie carried an extra twenty pounds on his six-foot-two frame, most of it muscle. Their shared broad nose and dark eyes marked them as siblings. Trey grabbed him into a hug, patting his back, always happy to see his brother. Even though their uncles had made a point of including them in family activities, they'd still spent a lot of their childhood alone due to their mother's rules. It had made the two of them close. Though three years separated them, they moved like twins, almost always knowing what the other was feeling.

"What it do, baby boy?"

"Ain't shit," Richie said, looking over the shop.

His brother had never been the outdoors type, instead spending a lot of their childhood in their shared bedroom on his computer. It paid off now in more ways than one. Richie had a lucrative career both on and off the books. With every sweep of Richie's eyes over the shop, Trey internally sighed. His brother was working up to tell him something.

"Spit it out, Richie," Trey ordered.

His brother sighed. "Remember you had me look into that bounty on Ness?"

Trey nodded for him to continue, bracing himself for whatever news Richie had to deliver. His little brother slid his hands into his cargo shorts and shook his head.

"Shit went up another million."

Trey cursed.

"As far as I can tell, no one in this area would even try to go up against the Fouches, especially knowing how our families are aligned. But—"

"That won't stop anyone outside of the area," Trey finished his brother's thought. "Three million is a lot of money."

"Not everyone will risk their life behind it," Richie supplied helpfully. "You know who this guy is?"

"By reputation only."

"What are you going to do?" Richie asked.

Trey shrugged. "Ness's family is aware, and you know they won't go down without a fight."

"Very true."

"All I can do is help them prepare." Trey's mind spun to all the possibilities that type of money offered would bring. Yes, no one in the area would dare try for it, but for that type of cash, there was no telling who would respond to the bounty. He looked up as he sensed his brother staring at him.

"What?"

Richie sucked his teeth. "What? You left me for dead with moms, man."

Trey snorted at the exaggeration. It had been some weeks since he'd last spoken to his mother, so he knew she was transferring all of her anxiety onto his little brother and his mate.

"Fuck out of here. She's your mom too. Some quality time will do you some good," Trey joked.

"She been blowing up my phone since she can't call her favorite," Richie whined.

"You'll be alright," Trey laughed.

Richie sighed. "Ness looks good on you, big brother, so I'll take the heat for now. Don't let that shit drag on too long, hear?"

"Oh, you giving me orders?"

"You know that old lady got me wrapped around her fingers. I hate when she's upset," Richie admitted.

"Richie, all she gotta do is respect my mate. That ain't even hard shit."

His brother nodded, conceding his point.

"She tell you the Colonel warned off my mate years ago? Not to mention, I just found out yesterday that she'd known Ness and I were mates from when we were kids."

Richie's eyes widened in shock. "That's...yikes. I didn't think she would come between a mating."

"That's what I'm saying!" Trey shrugged. "I'm not abiding by that shit."

"Fair," Richie conceded. "Okay, I'll talk to ma."

"Don't get in the middle of it, baby brother," Trey cautioned.

Richie sighed in defeat. "Alright then. I'm out. You need anything else from me?"

Trey smiled. "I want you to formally meet my baby."

"Let's do that." Richie returned his smile. "We can double date. I'll see when Tam is available."

"Bet." Trey pulled his brother in for a hug.

Trey returned to what he was doing, making adjustments where he saw fit. He didn't know how much time had passed since his brother left, but his wolf growled within him, pausing his work. He looked up, squinting as a dark-skinned man got out of a rented SUV, his curious gaze raking the shop. Tall and muscular, the power radiating from the male gave him away as a warlock. There was none of the wild smell Trey associated with shifters, and none of the other tells that he usually sensed from other paranormals.

From the stiff jeans that looked fresh out of the package and the obviously new t-shirt, it was clear the man was trying to go for casual — he looked everything but. That raised Trey's hackles, putting his wolf on alert. Trey put his tools down and folded his arms over his chest, watching as the man stepped into the garage. His uncle came out of his office, a blunt hanging from his lips, his nine down at his side. They both eyed the stranger. Trey narrowed his eyes, recognizing the body shape and gait. It was the same man who had been in the parking lot during the incident with the bear.

Up closer, Trey took in the male's features, committing them to memory, from the strong jaw and high cheekbones to his dark inset eyes. He had a suspicion of who the man was, but out of uniform, there was nothing he could do about it.

"What can we do for you?" Nathan asked.

"I heard this was the place for the best custom bikes."

Nathan said nothing, Trey taking his cue from him. The silence got tense, but no one was willing to fill it.

The stranger chuckled. "I was surprised someplace so far out of the way got a reputation like the one y'all have."

Again, silence.

The man turned to look at Trey, a slight smirk tilting his lips. "I see y'all aren't going to make this easy. I heard I could get information...and supplies out this way too."

"My man, unless you got a motorcycle in the back of that fancy fucking SUV, we ain't got nothing for you." Trey stepped closer, irritated with the male's smarmy presence.

The man's face hardened, then went back to its affable facade. "A'ight, you got it then. I got a friend out this way, Vanessa Fouche. Either of you know her or know where I can find her?"

"She your friend, and you don't know how to find her? Weird," Trey said and went back to his bike.

His wolf wanted to attack the man for simply mentioning his mate's name, but Trey never acted impulsively, so he swallowed his anger. Nathan returned to the office and left the man standing in the middle of the shop. No one else stepped up to help him until he departed. Trey watched him go, memorizing his license plate. As soon as the man pulled off, he texted dispatch to run the plates. He wanted to know where the man was staying. With the information Richie had given him, he feared their town would start filling up with people hunting down the three-million-dollar bounty on his mate. He went into his uncle's office.

"Car's a rental. Think you'll get something from the plates?" Nathan asked.

"Ain't too many rental places 'round here. I'll find something."

"You warning baby girl?"

Trey nodded. "Headed out that way now."

He hopped on the motorcycle he rode to the garage and hit the back roads home just in case he was followed.

Chapter Seventeen

S pending the day in and out of home stores was not on Ness's schedule for the day, but Dawn was persuasive, and Ness was too worried to bake, so here she was. At least she'd gotten some new kitchen gadgets out of the deal. Ness invited Bev mainly because she loved her cousin's wife, but she also wanted to reestablish their relationship now that she was moving back home permanently. The two of them had grown close even with the distance because she'd counted on Bev to get her out of many of her scrapes. Now that they would be living in the same city, it would be fun to hang out... outside of the police station.

"These have clearly been in somebody's house. The least they could do is cleanse the furniture when they get returns," Dawn grumbled.

Ness knew well what her mother was fussing about. There were several spirits clinging to a lot of the furniture in the clearance section. It was off-putting, to be sure, but Dawn could afford brand-new furniture.

"Mama, get your cheap ass out of the clearance section," Ness said, exasperated because her mother had been fussing for nearly thirty minutes.

And Ness was tired of warding off the spirits in this section. She was getting ready to leave her mother over here by herself. The store was a warehouse, an elegant maze of furniture and home accessories with plenty of space to get distance from this area.

"You act like you grown, and I'm not finna have it," her mother fussed, but she stormed off.

Ness gave a relieved sigh and followed the woman over to the brand-new beds. Bev trailed beside her as they watched Dawn examine furniture.

"Aunt Dawn is hilarious," Bev said, bumping her shoulder. "And you two have gotten along all day. Good for you."

"Thank God for therapy," Ness said. "The woman you suggested is amazing and has a way with her."

Bev smiled and clapped. "I'm happy it's working out. How are you and Trey doing?"

Ness's face heated. "We're fine."

"Is he still not talking to his mother?"

Ness frowned. "Wait...I didn't know that."

Bev nodded. "Yep. Aunt Val was talking about it with my mama the other day. Aunt Trice was upset enough that she reached out to her big brother. It's been going on for a few weeks."

Ness had forgotten how small the town could be sometimes. They were all interconnected with each other, making it so easy for rumors to spread. In this case, Bev was a Taylor, her father one of Trey's uncles, so of course, she was attuned to any family drama happening. Still, she was a little hurt that she'd had to hear about it from someone other than Trey.

"Oh my God," Ness whispered.

Trey loved his mother, she had no doubt about it. She hadn't realized their mating was costing him that relationship.

"Did Ms. Val say why?"

Bev gave her a look that answered the question better than words.

Ness sighed. "I'll talk to him. I didn't realize Ms. Patrice actually hated me that much."

Bev rubbed a hand over her shoulder. "She doesn't hate you. At least, I don't think."

Ness snorted. She needed to find a way to fix this. Trey brought so much to her life. She didn't want to be the reason he lost his family. She pulled out her phone and rolled her eyes when she saw that Trey had changed his name in it.

Ness: We should invite your parents to dinner.

She watched the dots appear and disappear for long moments until he sent back:

Baby daddy: We'll talk about it.

That was it.

Ness sighed and pocketed her phone. The hair on her arms rose, and she could feel magic gathering in the air. She looked around for her mother, needing to put eyes on her. This magic didn't feel at all familiar. Next to her, Bev started coughing and going down to her knees. She clutched her stomach a moment before her coughs changed to gagging. Ness gasped and called to Candace.

Her guide appeared instantly. *"There are two magic users in here."*

Ness cursed and looked for the telltale signs of magic around Bev. Finding the spell, she worked quickly to dismantle it. Her mother rushed to her side, and the room around them muffled as Dawn threw up a protection spell.

"What's happening?" Dawn asked, her eyes scanning the store.

Ness said nothing, concentrating on disassembling the spell. Her hands shook, but a few seconds later, she was able to take it apart.

"Someone is attacking Bev," she finally told her mother, looking around the store.

Bev took a deep breath, her body falling onto Ness as her legs gave out. She sat her cousin down on the mattress they were standing next to and rifled through her purse for the small bottle of water she kept there.

"Drink this," she ordered, resuming her scan of the store. "Candace says there are two magic users present."

"Find them," Dawn told her. "I don't want to take my concentration off the protection circle to talk to my guides."

Ness took a deep breath and sent out tendrils of magic. It was easy to find them since she'd broken down their spell. The taste of their magic was inside of her, and one thing about her power...she could give that shit right back to them. The spirits around them were malevolent, twisted like the magic user they surrounded, and Ness used them to amplify her reverse spell. Gathering more power from the neutral spirits lingering in the store, Ness lashed out with it. Candace gave her a nod of approval.

Loud curses sounded as one of the warlocks hit the floor a few aisles away, gripping his throat. Ness didn't recognize him at all, but she had no time to get a closer look. There was still one more person out there. She focused on the second one, her lips moving as she chanted. Some part of her worried that karma may come back on her for the spell, but she would always defend herself. There was a small scream as a petite woman scrambled from behind a partition. Her exposed skin was red and inflamed, the cold heat from Ness's magic searing her.

"*You need to go,*" Candace told her. "*They aren't the only ones coming for you.*"

She nodded and gripped Bev's arms, helping her stand. It was slow going as they shuffled through the aisles and aisles of home décor. They could've moved faster, but Ness was afraid that the two magic users were not alone. So, she was careful, keeping away from the staff gathering around the two people she'd taken out. When no one followed them from the store, she breathed a sigh of relief. Her heart was racing as she rushed back to Springbrook and the safety her family's barrier provided. She didn't drive straight home, instead taking a circuitous route, circling back when she could to make sure they weren't followed. She didn't breathe easy until they reached her yard. She frowned at the unfamiliar car.

Bev cursed. "Aunt Trice," she supplied.

Ness dropped her head to the steering wheel. She needed to talk to the woman but now was definitely not the time. They all exited the car, lugging the bags from the other stores they'd visited. She walked in and felt the tension immediately. Trey stood over his mother, the two of them staring at each other but not saying anything.

"What's going on?" she asked her mate.

Trey's jaw worked as he finally spared her a glance. "My mother came to apologize."

"This time," Trice growled, and Dawn — the shit starter that she was — scoffed.

"Patrice Harvey apologizing? Yeah, right."

"Mama," Ness said. She was getting a headache. It was from expending magic, but the stress and tension filling her home wasn't helping. "Let's all sit down," she said tiredly.

Patrice and Trey were still in a standoff, and honestly, Ness hurt for him. They all trekked into the kitchen.

"I'm gonna leave y'all to it," Bev called from the door.

Dawn turned and pointed a finger at Bev. "No, ma'am, go lay down on that couch while we deal with this. I need Shelby to look you over."

Ness wiped a hand down her face. For a brief moment, she'd forgotten about the attack. They still needed to deal with that.

Internally, Trey was cursing. He'd wanted to have his mother out of the house before his mate got home. He was already stressed about what he had to tell Ness; he didn't want to add Patrice on top.

Dawn broke the tense silence that had settled over the kitchen. "Let's hear this apology. I imagine it has to taste like acid."

"Jesus, Mama," Ness sighed. "I'll make tea."

The matriarchs stared each other down. The two women couldn't be more different. His mother towered over Dawn's diminutive stature, but Ness's mother's attitude more than made up for the height difference. They eyed each other, clearly something more at play than what was on the surface.

Dawn smiled, and nothing about the tilt of her lips gave amusement. "I thought you said you wouldn't step foot in my mama's house again."

"I didn't come here to argue with you, Dawn," Patrice said primly.

Dawn sniffed in disdain.

"Would you like something to drink, Mrs. Harvey?" Ness asked from across the kitchen.

"Uh-uh, don't be making her comfortable. After all the shit she's talked about me?" Dawn stepped in.

"Mama," Ness warned.

Dawn sucked her teeth. "Fine, I'll be on my best behavior for my son-in-law."

Patrice scoffed. "I wonder what that looks like."

"Mama." Trey gave the warning this time.

Patrice sighed and cleared her throat. Ness's eyes widened, and she shared a look with Trey. He needed to touch her and ensure she was okay, so he crossed the kitchen to be at her side. He slid his hand to the small of her back and pulled her into his chest. He closed his eyes, allowing her presence to soothe some of his anger. Something akin to panic and fear was lingering in his mate's mind, and for a moment, Trey wanted to kick everyone out and check in with Ness. Had something happened while she was out?

He thought about the warlock who had shown up at his uncle's shop. Shit, they didn't have time for this. But he knew his mother. Patrice was on a mission, and nothing would distract her from that. It was best to go ahead and deal with it.

"You've kept me from my mate," he directed at his mother.

Disappointment weighed his chest. He knew Ness wanted the conversation much less contentious, but he was down to the end of his patience. With the danger surrounding the town, he didn't have time to mince words with his mother.

"I've kept you alive. I won't apologize for that." Patrice pursed her lips.

"The curse is broken." However, that shouldn't have mattered.

"*Now*. It wasn't when you were a child. How could I give my firstborn over to this family knowing the fate that awaited you?"

Trey could understand and give her grace for that, but everyone in town had known the moment the curse was broken. Patrice had still been actively trying to keep him from even the chance of running into his mate.

"You still don't want me with her." It wasn't a question. He knew well her thoughts on the matter.

Patrice looked guiltily at both Ness and Dawn before sighing. "You saw her for the first time in a police station. Who knows what number visit that was?"

"Not too much on my goddamned daughter, now," Dawn snapped.

"Mama, let them talk," Ness told her.

He could feel his mate's hurt down their bond, and damn if it didn't piss him off. This was the exact reason he didn't want the two women to interact. He would do anything to protect Vanessa.

"I love her. That's it. That's all. I refuse to let you or the Colonel disrespect my mate."

Patrice lowered her head. "I don't want this distance between us, Joseph."

Trey ground his teeth but kept his mouth closed. His stance was unyielding. Their gazes collided, each of them stubborn in their own way. His mother needed to understand that he wasn't giving in when it came to his mate. She sighed and turned to Ness.

"I apologize, Vanessa. For my unkind thoughts and my part in keeping the two of you separated."

Ness nodded. "For what it's worth, I understand."

"When your grandmother told me that the two of you would be mates, I...panicked. I didn't want my son falling victim to the curse over your family," Patrice further explained.

Ness held up her hands. "Honestly, I understand. My cousins and I fought the curse in our own ways. I can't imagine watching my child get entangled in it."

Dawn scoffed but said nothing.

Patrice cut her another look but gathered herself. "Well, I'll get out of your way. Joseph, will you make it to Sunday dinner?"

He looked down at his mate, and she placed a hand on his chest and signaled that she was okay with it.

"Fine," Trey conceded.

Patrice nodded and left with that.

"Talk about a weird ass day," Dawn muttered.

"Who you telling," Ness said, leaning against the counter and wiping a hand down her face.

"What happened?" Trey frowned.

Ness shook her head. "Did you know about the both of us, mama?"

Dawn shrugged. "Those days run together for me, I'm afraid to say, my love. I vaguely remember Mama gathering Patrice and me together to tell us, but..."

Ness took a deep, shuddering breath. "Of course, I didn't think about that."

His mate was hiding something from him. The fear and panic slowly dissipated from their bond, so she was calming, but there was still...something. He cupped her chin and drew her eyes to him. She wouldn't meet his gaze, and he sighed. She looked exhausted but so very beautiful. His eyes traced her body, and his wolf got excited. She was his, and he liked that shit.

"What's wrong, mamas?" he muttered, nuzzling into her neck.

Her body was tight, but she relaxed when he reached out to the cat within her. Her heart thumped, and he put his palm against her chest.

"It's happening," she said softly, her fear spiking and riling his wolf.

"Settle, kitty cat, we're in this together."

She lowered her head to his shoulder. "Trey, I don't want this to hit my family," she whispered.

"We got you, Ness. I swear it to you." He kissed her, forgetting they weren't the only ones in the house.

Dawn cleared her throat. "No time for that, we got shit to do."

Trey sighed because she was right. All indications pointed to Zane having finally arrived in Springbrook, and they needed to prepare for that.

Chapter Eighteen

"**B**aby!" Marcellus busted through their front door, his eyes hectic.

Her aunt Shelby was right behind him, her canvas bag gripped tightly. Her eyes sought out Ness.

"Tell me."

"I unraveled a spell from around her, but I wanted you to check behind me in case any part of it lingers," Ness explained.

"What happened?" Shelby asked, rushing to her daughter-in-law's side.

"We were attacked in the furniture store."

"In town?" Trey asked, grabbing her shoulders.

She nodded. "I was coming to tell you, but then everything with your mother..."

"Tell me now," he demanded.

She rolled her shoulders, fighting the tension gripping her body. "A witch and warlock attacked us. I don't know any details other than that."

"What happened to them?" Cellus asked.

"I fought back. Last I saw, they were laid out in the middle of

Johnson's off of Atama Street. I didn't stick around to see if they were okay."

Trey cursed and pulled out his phone. He left the room, and Ness figured it would be to call his deputies. Candace hovered over Shelby as she worked. Nic came in the door with JT trailing her. Audrey was next, pulling a suitcase behind her. Ness knew that it was necessary, but she would miss her privacy.

"I got deputies on it," Trey said, pulling her attention back to him.

"Everyone's here," she told him.

"What's going on?" Nic asked.

She was already tired of telling the tale. She should've sent a family group text.

"We were attacked," Dawn answered this time.

"By who?" JT growled.

Her mother shrugged.

"So it's started?" Audrey asked.

Ness looked to Candace, who shook her head.

She hated what she had to tell her family. "No, this isn't Zane. I mean, maybe, but indirectly. This wasn't him."

Trey sighed. "It's the bounty."

Ness looked at him in surprise. "You know?"

"You know and didn't tell me?" he shot back.

"I...it slipped my mind. There is so much shit going on right now, Trey."

"A three-million-dollar bounty on your life slipped your mind?" Trey snapped.

Ness flinched, unused to him talking to her like that. Also, she hadn't realized it had reached that high. She shivered, knowing the caliber of people that would come after that type of money would get progressively more skilled.

"Three million dollars!" Audrey shrieked. She turned to her husband. "You didn't say it was that high."

"Monica warned me, and I didn't think about it. I'm sorry," Ness told them.

Trey sighed and paced away.

"That's higher than when I checked. When did it go up?" JT asked.

"Jesus Christ on the cross, does everyone know about it but me?" Nic asked. "Why didn't you tell me?"

JT turned to soothe his mate. "Ain't nobody foolish enough to run up in our shit behind no bounty. At least not at the amount that was first offered. I didn't realize it was up that high."

"When did you find out?" Ness asked Trey, tuning out the family for a moment.

"When I was searching your records. Richie hit me up today to tell me about the increase."

"So, you've known all this time, too," Ness pointed out.

He cursed. "I had my brother keeping an eye on it."

She sucked her teeth and turned back to her family.

"So not only is Zane after you, but now every weirdo wanting that money will be coming after this family," Marcellus snapped.

"I'm sorry."

"It's not your fault, Ness," Audrey soothed.

Nic held her hand up to stall any further arguing. "We'll strengthen the barrier, and Ness, you're stuck in the house until we figure this out."

"Excuse you, I'm not trapping myself in this damn house."

"*Ness,*" Candace chastised.

If Candace was worried, then it was worse than they thought. That, more than anything, made her relent.

"Fine," she snapped.

Her mate was silent, and she was almost afraid of what he would say.

"I'm taking my wife home. Will I need to worry about the kids going back and forth to school?" Marcellus's gaze pinged between them all, waiting on someone to answer.

Candace shrugged. Patsy was absent, and Ness was at a loss for how to reassure her family.

"My babies are protected," Shelby told them. "Don't worry about that. I suggest everyone up their protection for now." She stood to leave.

The room dispersed, and Ness was left with her mate. He was clearly still aggravated with her.

"You knew already, Trey. What did you want me to tell you?"

"I thought I was protecting you..." he started but then shook his head. "You cannot hide shit from me, Vanessa." He sighed, and his shoulders slumped. "I actually am not in the mood to argue about this shit," he said, walking away.

Ness was at a loss for what to do. Her family was in shambles, and there would be no running or conning her way out of the situation she'd gotten them into.

Storming out hadn't been the answer, but damn if Trey could stop himself. He prided himself on being even-tempered. His mother was high-strung, and he'd made sure that he was the opposite of that. But the riotous feelings stewing inside of him were ones he couldn't control. Logic was no help in this situation because there was nothing logical about the way he felt about that woman. Just the thought of her being in danger had his vision swimming in panic.

He'd long given control over to his wolf, and the animal had taken full advantage, running the woods until Trey could finally sort through the disjointed thoughts worrying him. Even after hours in his wolf's body toggling between anger at Ness and fear, he still hadn't come up with a solution that would keep her involvement minimal.

The animal was simpler in its thinking. His wolf wasn't worried.

Trey believed in his own strength and that of his wolf. He knew he could protect her...she just had to let him. And it seemed that was a foreign concept for his mate. It was frustrating, to say the least. He finally found a comfortable spot, and the wolf laid its body down. Hidden by the lush greenery around him, Trey watched the house that was now his new home. In his animal form, he could see the traces of magic as the people inside worked with it. It would take a lot for his wolf to get used to it, but he was willing to do whatever to be with Ness. There would be people in and out of the house; it was a part of how the Fouches loved each other. His wolf was resigned to that, but it didn't stop the animal from marking more spots around the property on their run.

It had been what the wolf was doing while Trey brooded, trying to find the best way to keep their mate safe.

He'd kept the bounty from her, fearing she would do something reckless, but that hadn't stopped her from being attacked. So, what it all boiled down to was that he was mad for nothing. It wasn't like he hadn't known about the bounty, but he'd thought he was protecting her by keeping it to himself. It hadn't occurred to him that she'd known and was keeping it from him, probably for the same reason. That hurt his ego some if he were being honest. He really thought he was doing something.

His ears perked up as the back door slammed against the house. Ness rushed from the porch.

"Trey!" She rushed outside, her eyes seeking him in the darkening evening.

He separated from the bushes that hid him and shifted, walking to his mate. Her eyes were wet, nervous energy agitating both their animals.

"What's happened?"

"They found one of your deputies," she whispered, a tear falling.

He cursed and raced toward the house. He grabbed his pants and stepped into them, pulling out his phone to see all the missed calls and text messages. Israel was there as Trey rushed into the house.

"What happened?"

"The warlock killed one of my deputies." He couldn't fathom saying that.

For so long, the town had been safe from this kind of danger. For it to happen on his watch brought him a special kind of guilt. He knew the sheriff's job wasn't necessarily easy, but he hadn't been ready for this. By the time his head popped from the collar of his shirt, his cousin JT and Israel were ready and waiting by the door.

"It's police business," he started.

"It's Springbrook business," JT told him. "Israel's repping the Fouches, and I got the Taylors. Let's go."

He nodded, knowing the men wouldn't be dissuaded. Eli was already waiting by the truck by the time he got outside. He growled because his wolf wanted to go a round or two with the lion shifter.

"I'm here in peace," Eli said, and Trey knew he didn't have time to play around.

By the time he arrived at the scene, most of his department was there, some in marked cars, the rest in their personal vehicles. Swirling blue and red lights lit the sky, but the sirens were lost as Trey's thundering heartbeat filled his ears. Word had spread quickly. Tears, somber faces, and even some angry ones greeted him as he got out of his truck.

"Sheriff!" his on-duty deputies called to him, headed his way.

Trey ignored them, instead pushing his feet to the cruiser haphazardly parked in the ditch on the shoulder of the two-lane road. It was clear the car had rolled into the ditch versus crashing. There was no front-end damage nor deep gouges in the dirt around the car. It seemed as though the uneven terrain simply stopped the car's momentum. The lights of his car had been turned off, so it was initially dark as Trey carefully picked his way down the ditch. Floodlights lit the scene a moment later, and he got his first look at the young warlock. Deputy Thomas was in the front seat of the cruiser, a look of sheer fear frozen on his face. Trey closed his eyes and said a prayer for him.

"What do we know?" he asked gruffly.

Another deputy stepped forward, his eyes red from crying. "He pulled over an SUV that matched the description of your BOLO and called it in. It was the last we heard of him. Dispatch got worried when Oliver didn't check in and sent me out here. I found him like this."

Israel was examining the body. His face was grim, and the power he was using raised the hairs on the back of Trey's neck. Trey looked around at the people who worked for him. Seeing fear on their faces did something to him. They had all been cocky in their ability to keep the town and each other safe. This was a blow to them all. He would make McIntyre pay for this.

Chapter Nineteen

The sun had barely crawled over the horizon, but Ness couldn't sleep. The coffee she'd made an hour ago was cold beside her, the damp air of the morning pressing in on the robe she wore over her gown. Trey had come in after handling everything with his deputy, and guilt had made sleeping impossible for her. She'd gotten someone killed. An innocent someone, from Trey's description of the man. Her heart ached, and from what she'd been able to discern from her spirit guides this morning, that was the least of what was to come.

She looked out into the yard; her family's legacy lay before her. From the garden neatly cordoned off towards the left with raised garden beds, to the long expanse of grass that reached the forest behind them. All of it was lovingly tended by them. The land had been in the Fouche family for generations, the women holding onto it through sheer grit. She was proud of her family and scared for what was to come.

"Don't tear up my garden," Patsy said.

Ness chuckled softly. "You've been missing."

"Time is so fleeting. Even more so on this side of the veil," Patsy said in answer.

Ness's stomach turned, her chest fluttering. She quickly changed the subject. "Nic will take care of your flowers and plants."

"Are you settled, baby?" Patsy asked.

Was she? Already, she and Trey were taking steps to make the house theirs. She was finally using her ill-gotten gains for something she could nurture. But she was reluctant to answer, already knowing what her grandmother was getting at.

Patsy hummed, taking Ness's silence in stride. *"A battle is coming, and I won't be around to see it, but I have faith in you. In all of you. Are you ready?"*

Tears clogged her throat. "Grandmother."

"It's time, Vanessa. All of you are settled, so I can now go meet your granddaddy."

Ness had gotten used to talking to Patsy. She wouldn't know what to do when she was gone. The tears she'd tried to hold onto dropped down her face.

"I trust Joseph to take care of you. Let him, baby girl," Patsy said sternly. *"Use every ounce of power at your disposal in this upcoming battle. Every ounce, Vanessa Fouche. No more being scared of your power, do you understand?"*

Ness nodded, a strangled cry leaving her.

"I love you." Patsy touched her cheek softly and disappeared.

Ness's heart knocked against her chest, the breath stolen from her lungs. It hurt all over again, grief barreling down on her until she wanted to sink into the dirt around her grandmother's prized garden. Hard steps sounded throughout the house, and Ness understood she wasn't the only one who'd gotten their final goodbye. She stood and walked back inside on wobbly legs.

Trey raced into the kitchen, his face groggy with sleep and eyes wild. "What's wrong, baby girl?" He pulled her into his arms. "I can feel you hurting."

"Grandmother's gone," she said into his chest, letting loose the sobs trapped within her.

"Oh, love," he said softly, hugging her tightly. "Was it time?"

She nodded, unable to stop the tears.

Audrey came into the kitchen. "She told you too?" she asked softly, her eyes red.

Ness nodded. Trey let her go, and she went to Audrey, pulling her into her arms. Nic came through the door, calling their names. The cousins clutched each other tightly, their grief filling the kitchen.

"She's fine," Ness assured them, wiping Audrey's face.

"I just got used to seeing her," Nic said quietly. "Did she warn you?"

The other two nodded.

"So, we should get ready." Audrey sighed. "I have some stuff in the workshop I gotta do."

"Me in the garden as well," Nic told them.

"I don't..." Ness looked around.

What did she have to do? She'd gotten them into this and was the least equipped to help. She shook her head and reminded herself of Patsy's words. She needed to come into her full power and stop being scared of it. For so long, she'd feared that she would end up like her mother or her aunt Kit if she let the power take over. Finding out that the two women had dealt with the consequences of a spell gone wrong should've reassured her, but it had done the opposite. The karma for dark magic was oftentimes swift and unforgivable. Ness hadn't wanted to risk it. But now...to keep her family safe, could she let go of the reins she held on her magic?

"You can help me find him," Israel told her. She hadn't even heard him enter the kitchen.

Her heart thudded because to do that, she would need to reach over to the other side. Patsy's words echoed through her mind. She needed to use all the power at her disposal. She nodded.

Trey cupped her chin. "No judgment, kitty cat. I know who I mated."

He was in her mind as always, soothing her before she even knew she needed it. She looked at the three men that she and her cousins had chosen. They each wore concerned faces.

She sighed. "Okay, but after breakfast. Are you guys hungry?"

"I could eat," JT said, going to the kitchen table. Israel sat down.

Trey grabbed her around the waist, resting his chin on her shoulder. "You want help?"

"I got it, baby. Sit," she told him.

Food was easy. It was all the other stuff that she was worried about. He still couldn't help her with that either, but knowing he would be there was reassuring, nonetheless. He kissed her neck, his wolf rubbing against her, and she got to work on breakfast.

Breakfast was long done, and Ness could procrastinate no longer. Taking a deep breath, she stepped into the semi-circle Audrey had drawn in the middle of the workshop she'd taken over. Of the three of them, Audrey was the best with spells, so they'd dubbed the workshop hers. Ness sat with her legs crossed in front of a glass bowl and nodded to Audrey to complete the circle. She shivered as her cousin's magic filled the space, the protection circle closing around her.

"You okay with this?" Audrey asked, stepping back.

"Just stay close," she murmured, not wanting to admit to the fear riding her. "Grandmother told me to stop hiding."

Israel shook his head. "What it must have been like to be raised with morals," he said bitterly.

Audrey rubbed his shoulder. Ness understood what he meant. From just the small glimpse of his grandmother they'd gotten when they broke the curse, Ness saw the greed the woman had. From Israel's stories, she'd raised him to think only of power and never the ethics behind using their magic. It had made Israel a dangerous and powerful warlock. Audrey had managed to tame some of his antics, but he was still just shy of gray with his magic. Really, he was the perfect person to help Ness with this task.

She was attempting her first peek into the other side of the veil. Part of her magic was seeing spirits in this realm. She'd never focused on those that were in between, having always been afraid to traverse the boundary of the worlds. Besides the fact that leaving her body empty was an invitation, she'd simply not had a reason. She was comfortable with her magic on the whole but more as a passive power.

"Remember, after an hour, ring the bell," Ness reminded her cousin.

Audrey held up the bronze bell. "I got you."

It was an artifact Ness carried around with her since she'd found it in an antique occult store. According to the shaman who'd gifted it to her, it was to be used if ever she strayed too far from her body. At the time, Ness had been still learning how to use her magic and had been giving thought to shadow walking. Just having the artifact and the shaman's warnings in her head had dissuaded her from it until now. Now, she would use it to help her family.

She slid her hands into the liquid in the glass bowl. Audrey had mixed a spell with the violet andisa plant, making the whole thing glow purple. They'd discovered their mothers had planted the first andisa, trying to amplify their powers. The purple one, in particular, boosted the connection with the other side of the veil and was perfect for Ness's current use. Her mother and aunt had used it to try and bring back Aunt Kit's dead husband, and that hadn't ended well for either woman. Ness banished that thought because she didn't need more fear heaped onto her and her purpose had nothing to do with resurrection. She prayed the distinction counted when it came to any backlash using the plant would have.

She swirled her hands in the mixture, power filling her body. She closed her eyes and slowed her breathing. Lowering her head, she covered her face in the liquid. By the time she lifted her head, the room was blurry. The bookshelves and their contents swam in and out of focus. A bout of vertigo turned Ness's stomach as she fought to acclimate to the magic. Panic tried to slow her for a moment, but Candace's image floated next to her, crystal clear, her guide ready to help.

Ness took deep breaths and focused, closing her eyes. A whoosh of air passed her face, and a freeing sensation overtook her. She opened her eyes and saw her body in the middle of the circle as she hovered above. The rest of the room was dark, Audrey and Israel mere shadows.

"What now?" she asked Candace.

"He's a bokor. Look for the unsettled souls," Candace suggested.

Ness didn't know where to start. Darkness pressed in all around her, tiny pinpoints of light here and there. In the distance, she saw the glowing outlines of humanoid bodies. Could they be souls? They looked so different on this plane. She frowned, trying to figure out how to close the distance between herself and the bodies. Before she could puzzle it out, in the corner of her eye, she glimpsed a procession of souls that were different than the others. Instead of an ethereal outline, their light was sickly, pulsing dimly.

"What's that?"

Candace made a sad sound somewhere between a sigh and a moan. *"Your warlock."*

Ness moved her feet, but she moved in place. Growling, she wracked her mind for a way to force her body to move in this realm. Instead of trying to walk, she leaned forward, smiling triumphantly as she floated along. She reached the souls and gasped in shock.

"What's happening?"

"He's trapping them. Building an army of the undead," Candace said softly.

"Show me," Ness demanded.

The fog between the realms thinned, and Ness saw Zane in the yard of a small cabin. His handsome, chiseled face held a coldness that made Ness shiver. Just on the other side of the yard sat a cemetery. He was reanimating the corpses, the magic leaving a sickly film along the barrier between the realms. Her heart hurt for the spirits being pulled from their slumber for his evilness. She needed to do something to stop him. But what? A song came to her, one her mother would sing when she was little.

Before she could control her magic, she would pick up all manner of spirits as she went about her day. Sometimes, she didn't have the resources to do a cleansing, like if she were at school, but there was a spell that would disperse the spirits for hours and give her a respite. The words were just out of reach, but in place of that song, there was always a baleful moan.

"If you do it, I'll be out for a few hours as well," Candace warned her.

Ness nodded, understanding. But doing it would reduce the number of "soldiers" Zane could make in the meantime. If nothing else, it would be worth that.

"Be ready," she warned her guide.

"Be careful getting back," was Candace's last warning.

Ness reached for her magic. It had a different taste and feel on this side of the veil, but she was able to grasp it. Pulling it into herself, she released a wail that had the hair on her arms standing straight up. Like a gong sounding throughout the spirit world, its inhabitants froze for a second before a wind whipped through and removed them from her presence.

Zane's eyes popped open, his hands frozen as anger transformed his face. He looked directly at her as though he could sense her nearness.

"Come find me, coward!" Ness called aloud.

Zane stood to his full height, throwing his hands out. Ness felt a heavy pressure on her chest, and she was pushed backward. She landed in her body with a thud, falling hard to the floor. She coughed, rolling to her side as her body ached.

"Shit," she heard Israel curse.

The power in the circle dissipated as Audrey pulled her magic back. Her cousin rushed forward, but Trey beat her, pulling her into his arms. Ness fought to catch her breath as she relearned how to operate her body.

"What the fuck was that?" Audrey asked.

Ness smiled, her eyes still closed. "I told that coward to come find me."

"Jesus Christ, you Fouches," Trey murmured, nuzzling her neck, his wolf reaching out to her.

It stroked her magic within, and her cat returned the greeting to her mate. Ness cupped the back of Trey's head and finally opened her eyes. He was still a little blurry, but after a few moments, her systems came back online. Her smile widened as his handsome face came into focus.

"There you are," she whispered.

"That scared the shit out of me," he admitted.

"Let me get a look at her," Audrey demanded.

Trey helped her sit back on the floor, and Israel handed her a bottle of water. She gulped it down gratefully, her mind processing all the images she'd seen on the other side. There was a lot of magic she needed to do to prepare. If Zane was building an army of the undead, then she wanted to be ready. She needed to talk to her mother, but she was feeling a lot better about the outcome. Yes, she had always been reluctant to delve into death magic, but she was born into it and would be damned if she would allow her fear to be the thing that brought down her family.

"I interrupted his spell, so he's pissed," she told them. "He'll be forced to attack sooner."

Israel turned to JT. She hadn't even realized he was in the room. "I'll need a place for a few people to stay."

"I'll make it happen. Trey, you'll need to leave your deputies out of this," JT warned his cousin.

"I'll still have them at the borders. I want to be covered if the FPTF tries to move on this town," Trey said.

JT nodded, and he and Israel left the room.

"How are you feeling?" Audrey asked her.

Ness examined her body and mind and nodded. "Scared, but I think I know what to do."

She shook her arms and hands, dispelling the residual energy left by the spell and the andisa. Her grandmother was right. As long as Fouche blood ran through her, she could handle whatever Zane threw at them.

Chapter Twenty

"N*ow!*"

Ness untangled herself from Trey and sat straight up, her heart racing. She looked around the dark room, spotting Candace immediately. She stood at the foot of the bed, her eyes wide with worry.

"He's working death magic," Candace told her.

Ness shook Trey awake. "He's here."

Trey scrambled from the bed and got dressed. Ness rushed out of the room and down the hall, knocking on doors to wake her cousins.

"Wake up!"

By the time she returned to her room, Trey was dressed, pulling guns from his safe in the closet. Her hands were trembling as she changed her clothes. They were both quiet, their thoughts their own, though the emotions running up and down the mating bond told of their nervousness.

"Meet you downstairs," she muttered, rushing to Audrey's workshop.

All last night, she'd been holed up in there with her cousins, working on spells that she thought would help them today. Her mother helped with some, and she was almost confident they would be what they needed. Zane controlled death magic way better than she did, seeing as how she'd never wanted to mess with it, but the counter spells that Audrey helped her come up with would go a long way to ensure Zane couldn't reanimate anything on their property. Now, that didn't mean he couldn't bring an army that he'd built. She'd seen with her own eyes that he'd been working on them. She just prayed they wouldn't have to fight an army's worth of zombies.

A loud explosion rocked the house as she hit the bottom step. Her pulse skittered, and Ness swallowed. Shit. It was starting.

Candace popped in front of her. *"The barrier is holding."*

Ness released a heavy breath of relief and rushed to the workshop. Footsteps thundered down the stairs, and the rest of the house awakened.

"Shit, fire!" Trey yelled from the front of the house.

Ness couldn't worry about that just yet. She needed to gather supplies. Nic and Audrey rushed into the office behind her.

"You got everything?" Nicole asked, stuffing the backpack she carried full of the spells she would need.

Audrey nodded, doing the same.

"I'm good," Ness told them.

The three of them shared a look, and Audrey grabbed them both, bringing them in for a group hug.

"We got this shit," Audrey swore.

Ness could only nod, the knot in her throat preventing her from talking. She knew the battle they were in for. She'd seen a glimpse of the magic Zane was capable of and wasn't as confident as Audrey, but it didn't mean she wouldn't fight with everything in her.

"Let's go," Nic ordered.

They filed out of the workshop and met their mates in the front. All of them were posted at the front window. Ness's stomach pitched. Fire lit the night sky, and she could only imagine what the warlock was doing on the other side of the barrier.

"Fuck this," Israel said. "Let's go, Audrey."

Trey opened the door and stepped out on the porch. The night was already stifling, humidity mixed with the heat of the fire pressing against her skin. The smell of smoke filled the air, and Ness felt like she was suffocating.

"Breathe, baby," Trey told her, gripping her shoulders. "This is your wheelhouse. I'm beside you all the way."

She nodded, gathering herself. "Candace."

Her spirit guide appeared next to her. *"West side,"* she supplied, already knowing what Ness wanted.

"He's on the west side of the property," she told the others. "Nic, you can thicken the woods there. Also, expect the undead."

"Like zombies?!" JT cursed, taking off his guns and setting them on the porch. He shifted quickly, shaking off his clothes and loping after his mate as Nicole took off for the woods to the left of their house.

Ness looked at Trey, if only to get her last dose of confidence before nodding. Trey had already taken off his own guns when she'd mentioned the undead. He shifted, a giant wolf taking his place at her side. She gripped the fur on his back and took a deep breath.

"Should we wait for him to get through the barrier?" Audrey asked, eyeing the burning woods.

Ness shook her head. "He'll burn the town down. We need to meet him," she determined.

They could wait Zane out, but in the meantime, innocent residents could lose a lot more than just their homes. Leaving a bokor on the loose in a place where their ancestors rested would be disastrous. To be slaves in death after the indignities suffered throughout their lives would be the ultimate disrespect.

"We'll circle behind him, box him in. Good luck," Israel said, kissing his wife hard.

The two of them took off in the opposite direction Nicole had run. She and Trey ran toward Nic and JT, Trey loping beside her in his wolf form. The ground was getting wetter the closer they got to Nicole. Her cousin was raising water from the ground beneath them to keep the fire from spreading. The tops of the trees were still burning, but they could travel through the forest without burning alive. Steam had the air around them scalding as they moved through. Ness's eyes were burning, but she couldn't stop.

All the practice sessions with her aunt ran through her mind, and she paused momentarily to put out the fire burning the tops of the trees.

"You don't have time for that, Ness!" her aunt Shelby yelled from behind her. "We got it." Dawn, Shelby, and Kit were rushing toward them.

"We'll be here, protecting the land," Dawn yelled to them.

Ness nodded, thankful for the added help but fearful for her family. She made her way through the woods, even as Nic's power thickened the brush. An opalescent waver in the air indicated that they'd reached the border of their land. What they faced took Ness's breath away.

Zane stood on the other end, rows and rows of animated corpses lined up behind him. It was strange to see the warlock dressed in slacks, a button-down shirt tucked neatly into his pants. For some reason, him dressing like it was just another day at the office scared her. Even scarier were the warlocks and witches standing with him.

It wasn't the United States Army, but with the number of people behind Zane, it felt close enough. She would almost rather face tanks and weapons. They would've been easier to defeat.

Fighting magic with magic would take everything they had.

"There's too many," Nic murmured.

The spells they'd cooked up wouldn't cover the number of animated corpses dotting the landscape, but they would do what they could. There was no other choice.

"We'll make it enough," Ness told her.

"Come out and play, little Fouche," Zane called out. "You've stolen from me, and I want what's mine." He held out his hands and threw his head back, a sinister smile covering his lips. "I can feel the power. It will be mine."

Ness ignored his taunting, instead searching the night for the signs of his spellcasting. He was animating the corpses lined behind him, which were her priority. Her cousins were supposed to take care of the rest. They were leaving Zane to Israel because, at the end of the day, he had the power to take the warlock.

"Come out from behind the barrier, and I'll spare your family," Zane called out.

"Why would we do that?" Ness asked, stalling for time.

The world around them shook with the sound of oncoming motorcycles. The wolves' paws pounded the ground, and howls rang out around them. The Taylors had made it, and the fight would commence in earnest. Ness took a deep breath and prepared for what was to come. Wolves poured out of the woods and immediately went for the undead as they'd planned. The big cats mixed in with the wolves shocked her, but she couldn't focus on that now. She knew Israel had something to do with it, so Ness put it from her mind.

Shots were fired as the Taylors on motorcycles took aim. It was now or never.

Ness pulled a purple crystal from her bag, praying they'd imbued it with enough of the andisa plant's power. She gathered her magic and released a baleful moan, the scream rending the air. It carried on the thick air and hit the undead closest to the barrier. They collapsed, the spirits being thrust from the decaying bodies. Some of the witches Zane brought slapped their hands over their ears, going down to their knees. Anyone using death magic would feel that cry. Ness screamed until she ran out of breath.

Once she was silent, the fighting resumed, the shifters thrashing at the corpses that were left. Trey lunged forward, and he and Ness rushed outside of the barrier. The more they could keep Zane fighting away from it, the less chance he would have of unraveling the border. Trey made a path for her, and she slung her magic, releasing the trapped spirits back to the spirit realm.

Her cousins were launching their own magic, fighting the witches Zane had brought with him. The ground shook with Nicole's magic, vines and tree roots snatching up a number of the warlocks, squeezing the life from them. JT fought beside his mate, his powerful animal the perfect match for her cousin. They worked together seamlessly.

Audrey used the fire around them, slinging it with precision at their enemy. The smell of burning flesh scented the night as screams filled the air. For every witch they killed, Ness sent their spirits on to keep Zane from being able to use them in his fight. The bodies were being burned, though that didn't seem to stop the warlock from animating them. It was a nightmare to watch one go down dead, only to rise again, parts of their bodies still on fire. Ness knew she would see it in her dreams for the rest of her life.

Trey was beside her as promised, attacking anyone who got too close while she did magic. His wolf was ruthless, his claws slicing through the undead, leaving nothing to come back at them. She looked around as more corpses popped up. There was some other magic at play. Trusting Trey to keep her safe, she paused in the middle of the fighting and closed her eyes. She sent her senses into the ground and finally found what she sought. Zane had bespelled the actual land, infusing it with his power so that anyone who had fallen would be reanimated under his control.

Ness immediately went to work to undo it. After a few moments of no success, she was frustrated. Audrey was better at dismantling spells.

"*Audrey!*" she called out mentally to her cousin.

Audrey looked up from what she was doing and headed her way. Eli was at her side in his lion form, cutting down anyone who stepped before them.

"What's wrong?" Audrey asked, out of breath.

Ness pointed at the glowing runes on the ground, and her cousin automatically went to work.

"I need more power," Audrey strained.

Ness was depleted herself, but she knew one source. She didn't want to disturb the ancestors on their property, but then Patsy's words went through her head. She needed to do what she could to win this. Digging deep within her, she reached out to the magic behind the barrier on her family's land. The ancestors answered, filling her with power until she was drunk with it. She could feel her mother guiding the magic toward her, and grateful tears trailed her cheeks. Ness touched Audrey's shoulder and supplied her with the power she needed.

Audrey released a relieved breath and renewed her concentration. Ness felt the moment his magic failed. Like a pop in the air, the corpses around them dropped to the ground, the spirits wandering, no longer tethered to the bodies. She needed to disperse them quickly before Zane had a chance to trap them again.

"Dawn and order, morning and heart, when spirit reaches dusk, from this world it must depart. Feel the sound of my voice, heed my hallowed song, and allow it to carry you to where you belong." She chanted forcefully, sending them back to the realm where they now belonged.

She looked around. Some of the wolves were down, but they were getting help now that the undead were done. Israel, Nicole, and Audrey had decimated the number of witches and warlocks. Only a few remained standing and fighting, and Nicole, with the help of her Aunt Shelby, was putting them down. Kit and Dawn were on the other side of the barrier, keeping it standing, protecting their land from Zane's magic. With her family's magic running through her veins, Ness wanted to end this once and for all. She searched for Zane, finding him standing before her mother, trying to work his magic on the barrier.

"Zane!" she yelled out.

The warlock turned to her, a triumphant smile on his face. He raised his hand, and Ness could see the hole he'd made in the barrier. The warlock closest to him slid beneath it, running full-on for her mother. At the same time, he aimed at Ness. The air was electrified, and Zane's magic slid through it. Before she could take even the smallest step to avoid the warlock's spell, Trey's wolf jumped in front of her, taking the brunt of Zane's magic. Through the mating bond, Ness felt the pain that inundated Trey's body as his wolf hit the ground. A cry was torn from her chest, and anguish filled her. She kneeled next to him, searching for a way to help him.

Fear and anger coalesced inside of her, steeling her for what she needed to do. She'd never tangled with death magic, but her rage overcame her fear. Gripping Trey's fur, she gathered magic from all around her, one single purpose in mind.

Audrey stood next to her and gripped her shoulder. Her cousin's magic joined hers. Nicole's was next as she raced to them, joining their hands. Together, the three of them directed their magic to the person responsible for the death and despair that had been brought to them. Raising her hand, Ness called down lightning, using it to strike down anyone standing near the barrier. She screamed her pain, every strike a penance for Trey laying still at her feet.

She didn't know how much magic she used, but the world around her soon dimmed and went dark.

Chapter Twenty-One

Pain bloomed throughout Trey's body, and for a moment, everything was dark. His heart raced with panic. The last thing he remembered was jumping in front of Ness as the warlock aimed his magic her way. He reached for his mating bond, finding it intact. He didn't know what had happened, but to know that his mate lived was enough for him. A wet trail of relieved tears traced his cheeks as her presence filled the bond between them.

Next, he reached for his wolf, reassured to feel the animal moving in his subconsciousness. That was another positive sign. For the amount of pain he was in, he discounted death. He couldn't be dead and hurt this much. He turned his focus to opening his eyes. Low murmuring sounded around him, tense and rapid. Whispering? He fought through the fog to see if he could decipher the sounds. His head pounded with his effort, so he gave up.

But he blinked, and that was a start. He bore down and fought to open the lids. A tiny crack of light pierced the darkness as he slowly lifted one and then the other. He wasn't able to lift them high enough to see anything in the room, but it was enough. The whispers sounded louder, as though his body had permitted his senses to start working. He still couldn't pick out the voices, but he considered it a win that he could understand them as voices.

He gave up on lifting his eyelids further, instead choosing to take stock of his body. What was working? What wasn't? Perhaps that was an easier place to start.

"Trey," his mate whispered.

The weight of Ness's head lay on his stomach, and he could feel her body shaking with sobs. He pushed past the pain to lift his hand. He was only able to barely touch her, but it was enough for now. Someone gripped his hand, and he could see shadows behind his lids as they leaned over him.

"Let me get to him, baby girl," a voice ordered.

His chest rattled with a growl as Ness lifted her weight from him.

"She has to stay near." That voice he recognized.

If his aunt Valerie was in the room, it meant things were bad. A warm tide moved through his body, and his wolf howled within him. The magic was heated, burning through whatever had a hold over him. His back bowed, and he moaned, unable to make more sound than that. A cool hand gripped the back of his head, lifting it from where he lay. His lips were pried apart next, and a strong, cold liquid was poured into his mouth.

That cold invaded his body, replacing the heat from moments ago. He choked, and his body was turned over right before he threw up. It seemed like a sigh of relief went around the room, the tension from moments ago lightening.

"Give him the rest so he can sleep," another voice ordered.

His lips were opened again and more of the liquid forced into him. He was spent by the time he'd thrown up for a third time. A warm hand slid against his forehead, signaling that they were done with that part of the process. He shuddered with relief. but he fought against the heaviness of his body, not wanting to give up conscious-ness until he could assure Ness he was alright. Sensing his worry, he felt her slide her cheek against his. Her scent covered him, and she tucked her head into his neck.

"I'll be here. I'm fine, my love," she whispered.

His body relaxed in relief, and he was out.

The air around him changed, and the pain he'd just been dealing with was gone. Was he actually dead this time? He was afraid to open his eyes.

"You're still very alive." The voice was soothing, amused.

Trey risked it and parted his lids. He smiled in recognition. "Ms. Patsy."

"Joseph Taylor the Third." Her smirk was so reminiscent of his mate that it clenched his heart. *"I'm very proud of you."*

The words filled his chest. "I'll take care of her, I swear."

"I do not doubt that." She moved closer to him, placed her hand on his forehead, and hummed. *"He got you good, grandson."*

"What happened?"

"Death magic is powerful, but dangerous and awe-inspiring. McIntyre tried to drag your soul to the afterlife before it was ready."

"They defeated him?" The last memory he had was jumping in front of Ness.

"At no small cost to y'all. But Zane McIntyre is no more, and the family has cleansed the land of all the evil he inflicted on it."

Trey breathed easier. He was sure there was more to what happened, but now that they had come out on the other side, there would be time enough for him to get details.

"Ness said you were gone," he whispered, remembering his mate's pain.

Patsy nodded. *"I couldn't allow her to lose you. But I'm on my way now that you're out of danger."* She cupped his cheek, her smile wistful. *"You two certainly took your time."*

He gave her a sheepish smile. "I wanted to be ready."

She shook her head. *"Had your mother heeded my warnings, you would have been years ago. But that's in the past. The future is waiting for you and my grandbaby, and I look forward to what you will do."*

"Thank you for preparing me for her." He now understood everything Nicole had been telling him about the protections she'd helped him with.

She chuckled. *"I'd hoped the barrier accepting you would've been your clue that you belonged on this land."*

"My wolf got the memo way before I did." He realized it was why the animal had been able to mark her territory with no issues.

"Goodbye, Joseph. Tell Vanessa that the garden at the house is not the only one she and her cousins are responsible for keeping. She'll understand."

He nodded, a lump in his throat as he felt her power sweep his body.

The next time Trey came to consciousness, he was able to open his eyes. The pain was down to a dull thump, and he could feel his body. He reviewed his interaction with Ness's grandmother, awed by the woman's power. He wished he'd spent more time with her when she was alive. His mate's scent was throughout the room where he lay. It took a moment to focus his eyesight entirely. He realized he was in their bedroom. The curtains were drawn, so it was dark in the room, a single lamp lit. Before he could panic, Ness turned her body and tucked against him. She was sleeping. Trey tightened his arms around her and took stock.

His wolf was more assertive, his senses back to full strength, though his body would take some time to get there. He rubbed his cheek against the top of Ness's hair, marking her with his scent.

"You're finally awake." His mother appeared at the side of their bed, her gaze worried.

Her eyes were red-rimmed as though she was crying, and she had her bible clutched tight in her hand.

"How long was I out?" His voice was raspy, his throat dry.

Ness scrambled from his arms. She reached across him and brought a straw to his lips. He took a few sips of water. She cupped his cheeks, her sleepy eyes roaming his face.

"This was the third day," his mother answered. She swiped a gentle hand across his head.

Ness closed her eyes, and he felt the touch of her magic in his head. She was examining him. She took a deep, relieved breath, and her eyes opened, wet with unshed tears.

"All good?" he asked quietly.

She nodded and tried to get out of bed, but he grabbed her arm, pulling her back into him. He closed his eyes and held her tight. It took a moment, but their heartbeats synchronized, and her emotions flowed down their mating bond.

"I was so scared," she whispered.

"It's late, so I will leave you two alone, but I'll be back in the morning. Do you need anything before I leave, Vanessa?" Patrice asked.

"No, ma'am. Thank you for waiting up with me." Ness moved out of his arms and hugged his mother.

Trey's eyebrows winged high in surprise. When had that happened? His mother leaned down and kissed his forehead.

"Don't scare me like that again, Joseph," she admonished.

"I'll try. I love you, old lady." He hugged her tight, allowing her wolf to soothe his.

Her touch still comforted him, even at his big age. Patrice's shoulders trembled, and Trey knew her anxiety had to be on ten. He didn't move, not even teasing her as she soothed herself.

Patrice cleared her throat and backed away. "I'll let the others know you're awake, but I'm not letting them in here until the morning."

She left with that, and Trey was finally alone with his mate. They stared at each other. It had been a close call for them both. He didn't know what happened once he was hit with the warlock's magic, but he would take the hit again if it meant protecting Ness.

"Come here, baby girl," he said softly.

She melted into him, sobs shaking her body. His heart thudded as he held her, his hands sweeping up and down her back in a bid to calm her. He murmured reassurances to her until her cries turned to whimpers, and she finally settled.

"I thought I lost you," she whispered, kissing him softly.

"I'm here, love."

She held her cheek against his, breathing him in. He did the same, sending more reassurances down their mating bond.

"What happened?"

She shook her head and looked away. "It took us a day and a half to unravel the curse Zane put on you. It was trying to..."

She shuddered and hugged him again.

"I talked to your grandmother," he told her to distract her.

Her breath hitched, and tears spilled from her eyes. "What did she say?"

"That the two of us are stubborn. And that the garden in the backyard is not the only garden you and your cousins need to take care of?" He studied her face to see if the words meant anything.

She smiled and cupped his cheek. "I know what she means on both things."

"She looked very proud that you and your family took down Zane."

"I was out for most of the end. According to Israel, once I killed Zane, they took care of the others he'd brought with him. They left a few for your deputies to placate the FPTF."

He nodded, happy to hear that. It would make his job easier when he was finally able to go back to work.

"The fire?"

"I wish you could've seen my mom and her sisters at work. Their magic is beautiful and so in synch, it was amazing to watch. I hope Nic, Audrey, and I can get to the point where our powers blend and meld like theirs did."

He pulled her down to him and nuzzled her cheek. "And you, my love?"

"I'm fine. I was out for a few hours with burnout, but I'm as good as new," she whispered, kissing on his neck. "I love you."

He hummed. "I love you, baby girl."

She settled her body next to him, reached her hand up, and pressed his eyelids down. "Now, more sleep for you."

He chuckled and hugged her tight, more than happy to let sleep take him.

Trey ran a hand over his hair. After a week in bed, he needed a haircut. Ness had offered, but while his mate had many skills, he didn't play about his hair, so he had declined. His body was still a little weak, but he was happy to be up and moving around. He looked into the bathroom mirror as Ness came in. She was still aggravated with him, but she said nothing, simply wrapping her arms around him and laying her head on his back.

He spit out the toothpaste and rinsed his mouth, waiting for her to start another argument. They'd been at it since yesterday. She objected to him returning to work, and he kept trying to explain that it was light duty at his desk. Hell, he wouldn't even wear his uniform. When he left the bathroom, he'd throw on a polo with the sheriff's department logo and go. For now, he was just in his jeans, his chest bare as he finished washing his face. She sighed, her breath brushing his skin. He shuddered as need slammed into him — that sneaky witch.

"Don't be coming in here to seduce me, Vanessa. I'm going to work."

She sucked her teeth. "Ain't nobody thinking about you, Joseph Taylor."

She said that, but her hand slid down his stomach, stopping shy of his unbuckled jeans. He closed his eyes and clenched his jaw because if she touched him any lower, he knew he would give in to her. Instead, he spun around, which was a bigger mistake because refusing her while looking into those beautiful dark eyes was harder.

She placed her hand over his heart, and the hum of magic in the tattoo was noticeably stronger as she pushed more of her power into it. She pulled back and nodded.

"I'll be fine, baby girl."

She didn't say anything, simply tiptoeing and grabbing the back of his head. Her kiss was initially soft, but Trey took it deeper, delving his tongue between her parted lips.

She pulled back, an impish smile on her face. "I didn't mean to start anything since you're going to work."

"I somehow don't believe that," he murmured, pecking her lips with a small kiss.

She smiled wider. "You want breakfast?"

He looked down at his smartwatch and hummed. If he timed it right, he could have his mate for breakfast and still make it to work in time. He could always get something else to eat while he was out. Making the decision, he lifted her by her legs and carried her to their bed. This would be much better.

Chapter Twenty-Two

Ness stared out the kitchen window, her mind everywhere but on her task. She'd lived the last few years of her life in constant anxiety, waiting for any one of her schemes to catch up with her. Now...what did she do? There was no looming threat of someone finding out her real identity, no family curse, no murder to solve, no warlock after her...nothing.

Just Vanessa Fouche and her own thoughts. Hell, even Candace had been quiet for the past few weeks. She and Trey had fallen into a rhythm and grew closer as every day passed. Almost losing him had put so much into perspective. It had happened a month ago, and she still got nervous when he left the house.

Everyone around her seemed to be settled, but not her. Not for the first time, she wished her grandmother was still around so she could talk to her. She missed Patsy and her advice. Ness had a tiny germ of an idea about what she wanted to do, but for once in her life, her normal capricious nature was absent. Instead of rushing in head-first, she was analyzing.

Some would call it stalling.

She straightened as she heard the front door open, shaking away her thoughts.

"It smells good in here," Trey said, sauntering straight to her.

Like he did every evening when he got home, he lifted her, kissing her deeply. His wolf's power brushed her skin as the animal reacquainted itself with her magic as though the two of them had been parted for days instead of mere hours.

"You're home early," she commented as he put her back on her feet.

"I missed you," he murmured, cupping her chin and kissing her softly. "What are you baking?"

"A cake for a lady at Titi Shelby's church," she answered.

"You been getting a lot of orders from the church. You should do something about that." He looked around, pouting.

She chuckled, knowing exactly what he wanted. Her mate had a sweet tooth, and she usually catered to it.

"You're spoiled." She laughed.

"I can't help that my baby be treating me good." He rubbed their cheeks together. "On the real, though, what you wanna do with this baking thing?"

She eyed him, warming inside. She had an idea that had been scaring her, but Trey was already gearing up to back her, and she hadn't even voiced it.

"Open a bakery?"

"Nah, you gotta put a little more bass in your voice when you say that. My mate ain't never been scared to go after what she wants." He nibbled on her lips.

Ness smiled. "I want to open my own spot."

She had waffled between that and going back into appraisals, but to her way of thinking, going back to her old job would bring the same kind of trouble. It wasn't that she was a compulsive thief, but the temptation to right a wrong would be too strong. It wouldn't take long for her to end up back dodging law enforcement. And with the Sheriff living in her house...that seemed like too much of a risky gamble. So, instead, she went back to her first love, one of the many things she was able to do with her grandmother. Though Patsy was no longer with her, she could almost feel her grandmother's approval.

"What you need from me to make that happen, baby girl?" He rubbed his growing erection into her.

"Just have my back," she said breathlessly, lust tightening her stomach.

"That's easy shit. What else?" He scraped his teeth down her neck.

"Patience. It'll probably take a lot," she murmured.

"I got that and more."

He kissed her, and her legs went weak. God, this man just did it for her. Ness pulled back from the kiss before they got carried away and lifted the cake dish, revealing the apple fritters she'd made him. He smiled, rubbing his hands together.

"You like spoiling me," he said.

She nodded. "I look forward to spoiling your big-headed babies."

Trey laughed. "Nah, they gone get that big ass head from your side of the family."

"Just for that, I ain't making you shit else." She busted out laughing.

"Liar," he said, lifting her.

He carried her upstairs to their bedroom, and Ness clung to him tight, so happy that she'd finally given in to Joseph Taylor the Third.

"I love you," she whispered against his lips.

"Forever and a day," he promised.

Epilogue

Five years later

November had been colder than expected, but by the grace of God, the weather had warmed just enough that having Thanksgiving dinner outdoors wouldn't be torture. Ness figured that if push came to shove, they could squeeze into their house, but between the Fouches and the Taylors, Thanksgiving dinner had become a big affair. The division of labor was traditional, with the men outside setting up the tents and patio heaters and the Fouche women inside cooking. For now, they were able to occupy their kids and keep them out of the way, but that wouldn't last for long.

Audrey sucked her teeth and put the stirring spoon down. "I just ain't made for cooking," she grumbled.

Kit laughed from the table over by the babies. "I done told you to come sit your ass down over here with me."

"No, she'd rather mess up the mashed potatoes to prove a point," Bev said.

Audrey stuck her tongue out and wobbled her very pregnant ass over to sit with her mother and aunt.

Dawn handed her niece a glass of sparkling cider. "You just gotta know your lane, niece. Now, when it's time to get the place settings together, then you can do that."

"You ain't got no business up anyways, stressing my grandbaby out," Kit fussed.

"Let it go, mama," Audrey grumbled.

"Speaking of stressing out..." Dawn started.

"Don't even start, Dawn," Lauren, Nicole's mother, said.

Dawn sipped from her glass. "I'm just saying. Another Thanksgiving with the ex-husband."

"Titi Dawn, leave my daddy alone. I'm not finna referee you and this one all night," Nicole fussed.

Lauren scoffed. "She need to worry about that married man she brought to dinner."

"Lord have mercy," Nic muttered.

"He is not married!" Dawn defended.

"At least not as of a week ago," Ness inputted.

Dawn narrowed her eyes at her daughter. "It's been longer than a week, and you damn well know it. Besides, they'd been separated for years."

"Cut it out," Nic snapped, slapping her hand against the table.

The room went quiet, the ladies sharing a look before smothering their laughs.

"Congratulations, niece. You didn't tell us you were pregnant again," Shelby said dryly.

Ness snickered, unable to hold it in.

"I am not having any more children," Nic snapped.

"That attitude says otherwise," Lauren chimed in.

"Three is a good number," Ness added.

Nicole narrowed her gaze at her cousin. "Just because you and Trey trying to populate Springbrook by your damn selves doesn't mean everyone else wants a bunch of children."

"He need to get off of her," Audrey said, eating the cookies Ness had set out for the older kids to snack on.

"Not too much on my babies," Dawn piped up.

Ness rolled her eyes. "We're stopping at four, thank you very much."

"Did you tell Trey that?" Audrey shot her a skeptical look.

Ness smiled wide. She loved her husband and would give him as many kids as he wanted. As though he knew they were talking about him, he came into the kitchen wearing a sweaty t-shirt and jogging pants. JT trailed behind him, looking equally disheveled.

"Y'all coming in here looking like y'all actually did some work," Kit teased.

"Papa!" Ness's daughter called, holding up her arms for her father.

Trey leaned down over their four-year-old sitting at the kitchen table beside her grandmother and kissed the top of her head.

"Daddy dirty, sweetpea. You helping Grandma?" He smiled at the messy rolled napkins their daughter, Nia, was working on with Nic's oldest daughter, Luna.

The two were born a week apart and were damn near inseparable.

Nia nodded, preening under her father's attention.

"I help, too!" their three-year-old Imani announced, never one to allow her sister her own shine.

Trey nuzzled their youngest daughter. "It looks amazing, princess."

"Y'all needed something?" Ness asked him.

Trey turned his attention to his mate. "Richie wanted to know if you needed anything before they passed town."

"We're good in here. Your mom should be here in a few," she told him.

"Okay." He leaned into her neck. She could smell the sweat on him, along with the scent that she loved so much.

"Get offa her! I got enough nieces and nephews," Audrey mocked.

Ness snorted.

"Not the pregnant lady talking," Nic taunted.

"Says the other," Audrey threw back.

"I am not!" Nic insisted.

"You gon' deny my son all the way to the delivery room, huh?" JT teased his mate.

Ness ignored their bickering, pulling her husband in closer.

"I just told my daughter I was too sweaty," he murmured, nipping her skin.

"I'm grown. I can decide for myself," she told him.

He kissed her. "I love you," he whispered against her lips.

"I love you too."

"Want me to take the boys for a bit?" he asked, referencing their twins, who were getting rowdy in the playpen.

They were in there with Audrey's son, who happily roughhoused with them. It was natural for the cubs, and Ness had grown used to their rough playing. They were barely a year old, yet they wrestled each other constantly, their wolves strong in them already.

"The tents are up and the tables down, so they can't get into too much." Trey sucked on her skin, leaving a mark and momentarily making her forget what they were talking about.

"They'll be dirty as hell," she told him.

"They can hop in the bath with Nic's demon."

"What? JT, I told you to keep that boy clean!" Nic growled and headed for the back. "And you left him back there with your father. Willie don't tell that boy no for nothing."

"Baby, leave the boy alone. Cubs supposed to be dirty!" JT called out, chasing behind his wife.

Ness laughed. "You did that on purpose."

"JT was out there talking cold cash shit about my smoked turkey. He need to be humbled." Trey's smile was unrepentant.

She could only shake her head. Israel came into the kitchen, and unlike his partners in crime, his chinos and polo were spotless and as crisp as when he'd walked into the house this morning.

"Now look how clean your son is," Dawn told Kit, snickering. "Ass probably ain't help at all."

Israel smiled mischievously. "I work smarter, not harder, Titi."

Using magic, he lifted all three toddlers from the playpen. They squealed in happiness.

"Israel, you better not drop my baby," Kit warned her son-in-law as he approached the table, leaving the boys floating.

Ness didn't even bother giving the man a warning. He would ignore it either way. Israel was determined that all their kids be used to magic. He gently set the toddlers down outside the playpen, which gave them the signal to take off. He shook his head and touched his wife's protruding belly.

"You two okay?" he asked her softly.

Audrey nodded, a dreamy smile on her face.

"I got them," Israel promised them, dropping a kiss on his wife's lips before deepening it.

His three nieces burst into a chorus of mocking smooches. He laughed, pulling back, kissing the three of them until they broke out in a fit of giggles. He pulled back and winced as something crashed in the other room.

"Iz." Ness shook her head.

He smirked and took off.

Ness tiptoed and kissed Trey's ear. "Mama's taking the kids tonight."

"Say less," he murmured, capturing her lips.

"Get out the kitchen with that," Shelby fussed with a laugh.

Ness looked around at her family, her heart full to bursting. It had taken tragedy to bring them all together, but nothing else would tear them apart.

Also available from Dria Andersen

Chasing Savannah One Night One Bite

Hers to Call One Snowy Midnight

Destiny Series

A Destiny Awakened

Destiny Revealed

Escaping Destiny

Haven Series

Haven

Soulbonded

Hellbound

The Hamilton Brothers

The Friend Contract

The Alpha Accord

Porsha's Wolf

Claiming April

The Knight Brothers

To Her Rescue

For Her Safety

For Her Protection

About the Author

I am a full time photographer, and a mom of two. I've been writing my whole life, and after the birth of my first kid, I decided I couldn't very well bring up a fearless human without first trying the things that scared me. So, I wrote my first book, and then subsequently more.

I try to write stories I love to read: love stories that feature brown girls like me. Some of my stories feature gods and goddesses, and creatures I derived from old, African folk tales remixed and thrust into a modern world. Visit my website, www.driaandersen.com for more information on my other novels.

Join my newsletter!